The Fire

My friend Freddy came to tell me about the fire at Butterfly Leaming's house. We raced to the scene on our bicycles, like we usually did when Freddy's dad's police scanner turned up any promising fires or car accidents. It was misty out, still early morning, and the air was full of thick, rank smoke. Fires always smell worse when it's wet out. When we got to the fire, the house was still standing, but smoke and flames were pouring from the windows and from holes the firemen had hacked in the roof. There were firemen from Woodbine, Belleplain, and Ocean View, as well as our own South Dennis gang, which was a kind of laughing stock among the local volunteer fire companies. The hole in the roof was to "ventilate" the fire, so the firemen could find the source. Of course about three quarters of the entire house seemed to be engulfed in flames, so finding the source of the fire didn't seem too difficult, but I'd never seen a fire yet where they didn't ventilate the roof. My dad says once they learn something at county fire school, "them boys won't unlearn it nor vary it for a million bucks."

Butterfly was an old guy, a little weak in the head, who lived alone and was kind of a hermit. I saw Ralph Hinson, a guy my dad knows, and he came up to me with his "I got some real juicy gossip" look and told me that nobody had located Butterfly yet. He said that Bobby Boyle, the guy who lived across the street and had called

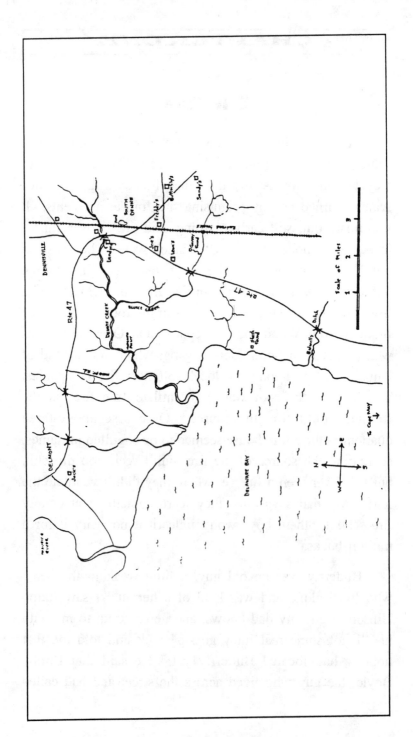

JOE BASS

Mystery Creek

by
Christopher Barry

To Jerry
Best Wishes
[signature]

Royal Fireworks Press
Unionville, New York
Toronto, Ontario

JOE BASS

Mystery Creek
Sneathen & Gone
White Wing
Mosquito Point

Royal Fireworks Press
First Avenue, PO Box 399
Unionville, NY 10988-0399
(914) 726-4444
FAX: (914) 726-3824
email: rfpress@frontiernet.net

Royal Fireworks Press
78 Biddeford Ave
Toronto, Ontario
M4H 1K3 Canada
FAX (416) 633-3010

ISBN: 0-88092-187-0

Printed in the United States of America on acid-free recycled paper
using vegetable based inks by the Royal Fireworks Printing Co. of
Unionville, New York

in the fire, had busted the door down, which was locked, and went in to see if Butterfly was still inside. But the smoke was too thick, and after two tries he had to give it up. Bobby was famous for having gone into the house that had been on this site previously while it was burning down, and saving a dog and a cat. That time the three occupants, which were Butterfly and his parents, were standing around outside safe. That was about twenty years ago, when Bobby was only about twenty-one or twenty-two.

Then Ralph said, "Where's your dad? Working on a Saturday?" Like the fact that Butterfly was possibly burnt to a crisp inside this burning house wasn't important enough to keep Ralph's attention any longer. I said yeah, he's working over Sea Isle, but I was disgusted with Ralph, and with most of the other firemen, who seemed to be having too good a time with the fire to worry about Butterfly.

"Maybe he got scared and run out in the woods somewheres earlier." This was from an old guy I'd seen before, but I didn't know his name. He was always at fires, though. At least he was thinking about Butterfly and looked kind of sad and nervous. Most of the other guys, like I say, didn't seem to care at all. He was probably in there, or what was left of him, where they were shooting lakefuls of water, hacking holes with axes and chainsaws, pushing in walls, and chattering.

My older sister Katie took Butterfly a plate of food and some cookies on Christmas. He told her about being robbed a few years ago, which was common knowledge, by two local boys who were caught when they tried to cash his blood speckled social security check, and how they went

3

to prison. Then he told her about getting robbed since then by a man he was sort of related to. He was too scared to say who it was, though he gave hints. He said this person hitch-hiked and got dropped off just down the road. Usually it was just after Butterfly got his check cashed, and usually at night. Sometimes he "would punch me right in the face," Butterfly said, and "he always laughed at me and made fun of me."

Katie believed him, but some of us wondered if maybe he was making it up. He did have the reputation for being weak upstairs. My dad said he was kept out of school because his parents said he was "different" than other kids. He had lived with his parents in the same house all his life till it burned down, then in this new one that was built in its place. Both his parents had died about ten years ago, about two months apart. Lately he used to sit at night in the dark, with just his little T.V. glowing bluish, scared that its light might attract robbers. After that first robbery, the one we're sure about, he didn't come out in the daytime for over a year. He'd slip out to Pedrick's store in the dark, just flicking his flashlight on from time to time, hoping to go unnoticed.

I knew his indoor plumbing gave up a while back. He used to go across to Bobby Boyle's every night to fill up two one-gallon jugs with water. And I had seen him slide out back of his house with a slop bucket once in a while, too.

Butterfly appeared to have been getting his courage back recently, though. He came out in broad daylight to get on the senior citizen's bus in front of his house and ride into Cape May Court House to go shopping at the Acme and Jamesway. I stopped once a couple of months back, mostly out of curiosity. He was pretty spooked at first, but since I was on my bicycle and was only fourteen years old, he relaxed after a bit. He was hard to understand. He mixed his subjects all up. "I don't know just why them boys done it. It weren't no amount of money to be going to no trouble for. But that one, I guess, he done it for sex." I don't know what he meant by that. Maybe he thought that the boy felt more like a man for beating him up. Butterfly was one of the palest, sickliest, scary-ugly looking guys you ever saw. He had teeth that were grayish-brown, with holes rotted in them, and some were missing, and a long, thin nose that had some craters in it. And real, real pale eyes, and bony hands with long yellowish fingernails and little scabs on them. He was kind of hard to look at, but I knew it wasn't his fault. I felt sorry for him. Butterfly talked about all kinds of things: people putting up fake surveyor stakes on his property, the price of cat food, people possibly stealing and eating his cats, and a lot of other things. He was pretty windy and didn't make a lot of sense. I was glad when the bus finally came.

Fred and I left the fire after a while. The ladies auxiliary—which is mainly the husky wives of the firemen, who wear those nylon jackets that say "So. Dennis Vol. Fire Co., Shirley" on them—were having a good time with the coffee and doughnuts and talking about fund raising. The firemen, excepting one or two, were having almost as good a time. We were disappointed and disgusted with them. When I got home, I told my mom about it, and she agreed with me.

What a way to start my summer vacation, I thought. Even though it was an adventure, it was a sad, depressing one. My mom told me there was a whole summer ahead, so look at the bright side. She also said, "people will disappoint you sometimes. And sometimes you'll disappoint yourself. But don't agonize too much over it. About halfway through the summer you'll tell me you're bored, like you usually do. By then you'll be looking for some adventure."

ᾶ ᾶ ᾶ

"They found him!" Freddy was screaming as he banged through our screen door. His dad has the police scanner, so he's always got the jump on me about fires and stuff. "They said his head wasn't attached to his body. Some said that. And he was on his back. Dad says in a fire they always go facedown, going for the air near the floor. And they said it was real burned near him. And he didn't have no 'Kero-Sun.' Dad thinks somebody set it, and killed him first. He thinks it was Billy C. Tobin."

"Now hold on, son," my dad spoke up. I knew he would. "It ain't such a good idea to come up with conclusions and mention names too hasty. I don't think your father would want you to quote him like that."

But my dad knew better. Freddy Chance's dad, Arnold Chance, was always very quick with a scandal or a rumor. He always knew them first. My dad had given him lectures before, which always made me feel funny when I went over to Freddy's afterwards, and I knew he would this time. My dad was big on lectures. I know they think he's a pain in the neck over at the School Board and Township Committee meetings. But nobody likes to say so, worried he might hear about it.

CHAPTER TWO

The Investigation

In the next few days I found out that Freddy's old man wasn't the only one who thought Billy C. was behind Butterfly's death. Down at Tommy Holmes' store in South Seaville and here at Pedrick's store in South Dennis, a lot of people were talking about it. Also at Ed Champion's garage and over at the sand plant, the men always seemed to be speculating about it. And the kids all talked about it. But Billy C. didn't seem to care. He was always popping up at the stores, especially Tommy Holmes', and acting like he didn't know or care anything about it.

Billy came from a big family of Tobins over in Ocean View. None of these Tobins was any good, but Billy had to be the worst. He must have been right around twenty years old, and he never appeared to have a job. He was stocky, but not too tall, and he always seemed to have crutches or a cast on his hand, or maybe a bandage somewhere. And he often had a slight grin on his round face. He didn't really seem dangerous, but I still stayed well clear of him, because he didn't quite seem undangerous either. My dad said he was no good. He always walked or hitch-hiked—never had a car. He had been hit by cars, though, some say on purpose, and once by a motorcycle. Freddy's dad said it was a shame his skull was so thick. He had real straight brown hair, which he combed straight down, and it looked as if somebody, maybe his old man, went around with a pair of scissors and chopped off everything over a certain length.

I never had much to do with him, as I've said, but a couple of days after the fire he came up to Freddy and me at Dennis Creek where we had a boat. Our boat was a little plywood garvey that sat upside-down at the landing for years. Nobody ever touched it, so finally we painted it and turned it upright and rolled it into the creek. When we launched it a few thousand surprised termites came scurrying out of the wood as the boat filled up with water. We left it sit for about a week, then bailed it out. It swelled up some, but it still sank if you didn't bail it regular, so I knew we wouldn't be allowed to use it if our parents knew about it. That's why we never told them.

The creek is about 50 feet wide where we had our boat, which is right near the Highway 47 bridge, on the border of South Dennis and the next town, Dennisville. It runs out seven or eight crooked miles to the Delaware Bay, getting wider as it goes. I had never been more than a couple of bends down the creek, though my dad had been down it many times.

We had two oars for the boat, a little dry-rotted, and different in length. They were under the boat when we first tipped it up. You couldn't pull too hard on them for fear they'd break, but we still had high hopes of going all the way to the bay someday.

At one time there were lots of boats at the landing, but now they were just sunken hulks. There was a restaurant and a house. But the house was empty, and an old guy named Popeye lived in the back of the restaurant, which still said, "Popeye's" on the front, though it had long since closed. That was over on the north, or Dennisville, shore and had a lot of bushes and reeds around it. Popeye was the only person for a mile in either direction, and he didn't see much from where he was, nor seem to care about it. So the creek was kind of our own little river, since people passing by in cars didn't even seem to look, and only occasionally did a strange boat or recreational crabber appear at one of the rickety docks.

Anyway, that day we were kind of sorry it was so private when Billy C. Tobin walked by and saw us bailing out our boat. He said, "This your dock?"

I said "Not really, Billy, but nobody seems to mind."

"How about the boat?"

"Yeah, that's ours," I said.

"Where'd you get it?"

"Found it," I said.

"Bought it," Freddy said, "Joe's dad found it and bought it over Sea Isle. " Freddy was pretty fast on his feet.

"You boys want to take me for a ride?"

"Ain't got a motor," I said.

"Then row, boy, row."

We were too scared of him to say no, but I knew it was a bad idea. Billy C. just hopped in and said "let's go."

I took up the oars and Freddy sat up front, which left Billy in the back facing me. The tide was coming in so that it was hard to make headway, especially with all the weight. Billy was good natured enough, though, but he wasn't having much fun with my feeble rowing. "Let me off anywheres," he said.

We landed about fifty feet from where we left off, but over on the Dennisville side, because it was handy, and Billy got out and started walking back toward the highway.

"I'll bring you boys an outboard. How much money you want to spend? My uncle rents boats over Sea Isle. I'll get one from him. How many horse you want?"

"My dad's getting us one," I said, trying to head him off.

"Yeah, I bet he is. I'll bring you one. You can pay when you can afford it. About ten horse be good?"

"He knew you was lying," Freddy piped up after Billy was good and gone. "Now what are we gonna do when he brings us one?"

"Well, I doubt he will. He'll probably forget about it. He was just talking big. It was kind of scary, though. He don't seem like a killer, really, but he don't seem quite right, either." We were shaken up by this episode, and we thought the best thing to do might be to stay away from the creek for a week or so and hope Billy C. would get picked up and put in jail in the meantime, as he often did, or at least lose interest in the project.

Freddy mentioned Leon Berman, a boy our age who lived in a big old house with his grandparents and his great-aunt Thelma, and was kind of a sissy. It wasn't his fault—he was an orphan, and these old folks watched him like he was made out of glass. He always wanted us to come see him. He wasn't allowed off his property much, and not having any brothers or sisters, he tended to get lonely. We usually came up with an excuse for not going over, which would make us feel bad for a while, but we generally got over it. The trouble was that it wasn't much fun to go over and have those old biddies breathing down your neck ready to nail you with a flyswatter or send you home if you got a little out of line. They were always afraid us "rough" boys would hurt Leon or break his stuff if they let us out of their sight for a minute. Sometimes if I went over by myself the old bats relaxed a little, but most of the time Freddy was over my house or I was over at his so that took care of that. But Leon was actually a pretty good guy, though, so this time we decided to brave it and ride on over.

When we got there, to our surprise, Leon was outside. He was with his "Pop," as he called his grandfather. They were trimming the hedge, or at least Pop was, and throwing the trimmings in the little trailer behind his tiny yellow "cadet" tractor. Pop was very proud of that cadet, even though it was really just a riding lawnmower in the shape of a tractor. It had attachments for plows, discs, cultivators

13

and stuff, but my dad says it would have a hard time keeping up with a roto-tiller.

It was nice to see Leon outside, but it wasn't real relaxed with Pop right there—we couldn't really talk about the things we normally would—so we just helped pick up the hedge trimmings. After we were done, Pop gave Freddy and me each a dime. We asked Leon to come to Pedrick's to get a soda with us. (Pop probably thought that was still how much a soda cost) but his Pop said, "no, we got plenty of soda here." Which I noticed he didn't offer us any of. So we just left, and Leon looked kind of sad.

"One of these days we gotta break him outta there," Freddy said, "if only just for the day."

"Yeah, I'd'a stayed longer, but I think we about wore out our welcome. Did you get the feeling Pop'd had enough of us?" I said.

"They never want you to come in the house when there's more than one. That's why he gave us the dimes, to let us know we were done. Leon might be a pretty cool guy if he could get out and around a little bit. Wouldn't look so pasty," said Freddy.

"Well, before the summer's over maybe my mom can talk his Granny into letting him stay over one night."

"That'll be the day," Freddy said.

彤   彤   彤

The next day, when my dad came back from Woodbine, he said a big old skiff was tied up at the creek, right up near the bridge on the Dennisville side. Looked like a crabber or a gillnetter, he said. This sounded like adventure to Freddy and I, so straight back to the creek we went, forgetting our strategy of staying away from there in an instant.

And it wasn't just a skiff. It had a cabin and was twenty-eight or thirty feet long. And there was crab shells and fish scales all over the deck. It was a big lapstreak boat with a cabin towards the front that had no back to it, so you could see right through to the windshield. A boat like that could get to the bay in twenty minutes, we figured, and what a trip! Rounding those bends, throwing a big wake, past the little islands, past Mosquito Point where old ladies were always crabbing, out to where the creek gets real big, then right out into the bay. They say the creek's three hundred feet wide out near the mouth. My mind was swimming, thinking about charging right out into the ocean when an old Ford station wagon pulled up.

"Get your grubby hands away from my boat!" A skinny old man had jumped out of the car, looking like he was about to blow a gasket.

"Stop where you are! What have you stole off my boat? I'll have the law on you. I'm a-calling the troopers!"

Freddy looked white a as a ghost. I probably did, too. I was having such a good time looking at the boat—the best boat I'd ever seen in the creek—then he came along and knocked the legs out from under me. I was scared but kind of mad, too. Freddy and I always got blamed for everything that went wrong at the creek. Like when Elmer Bolger's boat sank. It was a pretty, varnished inboard speedboat. Fred and I were very happy when it showed up at the creek. It really added glamour to the place. It wasn't there a week when somebody who didn't like Elmer pulled the plug, and down she went. We told my dad right away, and he drove us straight over to Elmer's to tell him. Elmer didn't say anything to my dad, but you could tell by the way he looked at us he thought maybe we did it.

"But we were just looking," I said to the old man. "It's our favorite kind of boat." I knew that sounded stupid, but it was all I could think of. The old buzzard got right in my face and told me I had no business anywhere near the creek, and if he caught me there again, I'd be in trouble with the law, and him too. His four front teeth were missing on top and he kind of spit when he said certain words, which made it all the more unpleasant. I knew there was no law against just being near the creek, but I also knew it wasn't a good place to be seen if something went wrong there, either. He cooled down a little bit as he went on. He probably knew he came down a little too hard at first. I told him my dad was Joe Bass, Sr., and I was Joe Bass, Jr., and that Freddy was Freddy Chance, both so he could tell I wasn't hiding anything, and so he knew that if he went too far, he'd have more than just two young boys to deal with.

After the old man left, it was hard to feel the same excitement about the boat being there. I hadn't pictured such a person owning it. And it was made by Clem Troth, Freddy and my favorite boat builder. We had never met him, but my dad had, and he said his were the best boats made. But when I thought of the boat, I thought about the

16

old man, and it wasn't a very good mixture. So Freddy and I decided not to think about boats for a while, and instead to investigate the death of Butterfly Leaming. It had been big talk for a time, but now people seemed to have forgotten about it. The "Police Line—Do Not Cross" ribbons were starting to tatter and fall down around his house. It didn't seem like anyone would mind us mounting a little investigation of our own.

It put a chill in me when we started creeping around the house—"the house of death" Freddy called it. The wet, smoky smell was still strong. The yard around the house was green and peaceful, though a bit trampled by firemen. Most of the walls were still standing, and inside it was scary and dirty. The black soot stuck to everything, except the metal stuff like the bedspring and toaster, which were already rusty and soft looking, like they were a hundred years old. Some of the books and magazines were in fairly good shape. They were charred around the edges, and damp, but the pages were intact, though they fluttered away in the breeze when you turned them because the bindings were brunt through. The one I looked at was "Reader's Digest Condensed Book—Gulliver's Travels", but it didn't have a cover—even a charred one. I wondered if Butterfly had read it, or the other books. Or if he could read at all. Or had they been left from his parent's days? "He had a sister who was a teacher before she died," Freddy said. What had been his little T.V. was now a charred screen perched on a little pile of melted plastic. About a hundred feet back of the house, and out of sight because of the bushes, was the place where he had taken his slop bucket to dump. And what a pile he had built up! I had never

17

imagined how high it could get, just occasionally seeing Butterfly traipsing out back with a single bucket as I did. Or how much toilet paper was involved.

We decided to head over to Pedrick's for a cola, and then sit down in private and go over the evidence we had gathered. Freddy had brought a notebook, which he had in his bike basket, and so we decided to write stuff down in a list so we could keep track of it. But all Freddy could talk about was Butterfly's "sewerage pile" as he called it. He wrote down how big he thought it was—a dumptruck load—and how far it was from the house, and then we got down to evidence, which didn't seem like much yet, about the crime and Butterfly. Here's what we wrote:

1. He was scared of people.
2. He had a huge sewage pile.
3. He had no running water to put out a fire.
4. He had no kerosene heater.
5. People said the fire was set.
6. He had a lot of cats, which were still around, though they laid low, and unfortunately couldn't talk.
7. He had been robbed before.
8. He had told my sister about a robber who could be Billy C.
9. The guys who robbed him the first time were out of jail, and so were also possible suspects.

Once we had the list, we sat back for a while to see if any ideas popped into our heads. We didn't want to tell anybody about our investigation yet, though. Our parents would warn us to stay away from the fire scene if we told them, and other kids wouldn't take it seriously and might mess things up. We could see that we didn't have much to work with, but there was no real rush. We decided to wait a couple of days and see if anything turned up or we got any ideas.

The investigation did take our minds off the old man at the creek and the boat ride with Billy C., and that was a benefit. Before too long we felt brash enough to take a ride down to the creek and look around. When we got there, we saw that the old man's car was there and his boat was out. We bailed out our garvey and decided to take a little row. Mainly we hoped to catch a glimpse of the big boat underway. The old man could hardly get mad at us for just rowing around. Our garvey was pretty creaky, but since the creek wasn't very wide, I knew we could make it to either shore quickly if she developed a drastic leak all of a sudden. Freddy said let's go to Sluice Creek bend, which is a mile down the creek, but I said let's just go a couple of bends and see how we do.

CHAPTER THREE

Old Jack

It's always a different feeling when you get a bend or two down the creek. It's like you're in your own world, different from everything else, instantly familiar, like you own it, even though it's something you can hardly picture when you're not there. The look and smell take over your mind. Your back starts getting sore from rowing or bailing, and not having a back to your seat. And I always think about how nice it would be to have a motor. Then the wind and the tide wouldn't mean anything because it would take no effort to overcome them.

I was rowing and Freddy, was bailing when we began to hear voices, like somebody was having an argument. Then "chink-chink" every once in a while. I stopped rowing to listen. I could now tell it was only one voice. It was a long bend with tall marsh grass, and we couldn't see to far around it. I handed Freddy an oar and we both paddled (so the oarlocks wouldn't squeak) because we were losing ground with the tide coming in. When we went a little ways you could see the back of the big boat—it appeared to be anchored or tied to something over near the right hand bank. The skinny old man was in it, kind of hunched, with his back to us, and the engine box was tipped up. He had his hands on his hips and stood perfectly still as we paddled toward him. I guess Freddy wanted to turn around and let the old man hang, because he stopped paddling. But I knew you were always supposed to help a stranded vessel, even a Russian.

I said "Boo!" I figured at least he deserved that.

"What the hell do you want!" The old man spun around when he heard me like he'd been stuck with a pin.

"You alright?" I asked.

"With a certainty, I ain't, boy. I got a chest full of tools and parts on this floatin' pile o' termite food, but I ain't got even one extra set of points. I tried cleanin' these with m'knife, but there just ain't nothing' there. Ain't you boys the ones that was messin' with this boat? You didn't have the key on, did you? That'll burn the points right up if they're closed at the time. "Course you didn't—I don't leave the key in her. I see you're yachtsmen, too. As a gesture of fence-mendin', maybe you two young bucks could row back and tell somebody to give me a tow, if there's anybody to tell. 'Course, I got a set of points in my car, I b'lieve, or if not I could go get one, if you boys was willin' to give me a lift back out once you give me a lift on in."

"The hell with you, buddy. You can swim back," said Fred. "We might tell somebody we seen you out here if we cheer up enough on the ride back, but that's it. After the crap you give us, we ain't takin' you nowhere."

I admired Freddy's guts, standing up to this guy, but I knew we had to help him. It's the rules of the water, which Freddy wasn't too familiar with.

"Well, boys, you got any favors owed to you? I was mighty rough and maybe jumped to conclusions a couple of days back. Maybe you was just nosy. I know there ain't much traffic out here, so I guess you got me by the short hairs. You give me a lift, and I'll owe you a favor. When I say it, I mean it. It mayn't sound like it's worth too much now, but when it comes up, you might be surprised how handy it is. It don't feel good beggin', but you got me fair and square. When you gotta eat crow, don't nibble, as they say."

We took turns rowing back—Freddy and I, that is. The old man said his back wouldn't let him, nor his emphysema. When we got to his car, he started rooting through the mountain of junk in the back, finally coming up with a set of points he thought was good enough to run the boat. All the time he was looking for them he told us a story about each thing he picked up. There were car parts, boat parts, T.V. parts, radio parts, airplane parts—I could see why the car had such a low slung look to it.

The row back was tougher with the tide still coming in, but "Ole Jack," as he told us to call him, was softening up towards us. I guess he was glad to have somebody to talk to because he turned almost friendly after a while, and every so often when he got going good, he would spit through the gap where his teeth used to be without meaning to, just like when he was yelling at us that first day. It seemed like he had done almost everything for a living in his day, and as old as he was, I guess he'd had time to. And this guy could talk more than anyone else I'd ever met.

"There was a time, boys, when I was hauling logs from down Delaware state. Let this serve as a warning. Do not drive through the state of Delaware overloaded. I was pulled into a weight station—'course I was overloaded—tandem homemade trailer, single axle Jimmy tractor with a worthless Toro-flow diesel, grossed out at over 70,000 pounds. The limit was about 60,000 pounds for a single axle trailer. Mighty low on funds I was, and greasy, due to repairs I'd had to make. Well, they arrested me. Here I was, a man forty-three years old, throwed in jail with chicken thieves. And the lowest form of life they was. The kind of people that don't register cars. Insurance? They never heard of it. Oh, I knowed these people well, boys, I lived down there around them for eleven years. They don't build houses, these people. They get an old wrecked house trailer and paint it silver. Not a mobile home, mind you. No, the kind you go campin' in. Though nobody's gone campin' in these ones recently. They paint it all over with silver roof sealer. They put concrete blocks under one corner, a couple of tire rims under another. Maybe a bumper jack or stump for the other two. They got plenty of bumper jacks. It's their favorite and commonest tool. This keeps the trailer from rockin' too badly. They stack up more blocks for front steps. Then they usually go to buildin' an addition. Beanpoles, corrugated tin, plywood road signs, and tarpaper being their most used materials. The dog and his family live under the trailer, or else in a fifty-five gallon oil drum with a door thoughtfully chiseled out of one end. They go down to the store for groceries. Not the supermarket. The little general store down at the corner. Outside of an occasional muskrat in the winter, and a few homegrown vegetables in the summer, they live mostly on un-nourishing foods. They give the kids potato chips for dinner, and the baby gets a bottle full of Pepsi, and maybe a cigarette if he finishes. They don't wash their clothes. They throw them in a pile when they get too stiff to wear till they've made a bet outta them. Then one day somebody with a college education comes around and tells them they need a better sewage system. Sewage system—you mean out house? Pitcher-pump? Then the cops come and tell them their boy's in trouble. Would they come bail him out? 'Bail him out? All his friends is down there. He wouldn't never forgive me!"

"These was my cell mates, boys. And none too particular about their housekeeping', even in them close quarters. Bath time was a community shower, courtesy of the guards and a fire hose. No sir. Do not drive through the state of Delaware overloaded.

"That was before I lived in Trenton. Lots of little colored kids around up there. Well there was colored adults, too, of course. I used to work in a big Quonset hut repairin' crop dusters—Stearman's mostly, which I also flew. There was a little alley behind our building, and a big warehouse across the street. Down at the end was a big commercial bakery, Bond Bread or somethin'. Well, every day a flour truck backed down this alley and unloaded, then drove out again. It was a real big one— looked like a ready-mix concrete truck. One day we was workin' and heard a commotion and some sirens after that truck had come and gone. We walked out to the alley and seen some cops and people standing around something.

Something not very big. Then right at our feet, we seen a small, flattened pile of rags in a mud puddle. Then we seen there was a lot of blood in the muddy water. All at once we knew that all them people was standin' around a little colored boy's head. He wasn't no more than five or six. And two little flat shoes. They said he must of jumped on the flour truck as it was pulling out, behind the cab, and fell off. Both sets of tires run him over. Blew his head right off, and it rolled a ways. The driver didn't know it happened, so we told him the next day, in case no one else had...."

It was a very revolting story, that last one, but he did a good job of telling it. It was harder to hate him after you got to know him. He told us more by the time we got to his boat. He told us his name was Jack Pugh, he was in World War II, though he was too old to enlist, and was "shot by an Eyetalian" over there, he had a "Delmont divorce" (him and his wife lived in the same house, but basically had nothing to do with each other), had owned a sixty-five foot oyster boat in the 1950's, had lost it during the oyster blight, used to fly crop dusters, had crashed one when an oil line broke and was in the newspaper for it, had to give up crop dusting because his eyes weren't good enough (he had clipped an electric wire with his landing gear is how he knew), but still had his old plane, had had a sawmill, was electrocuted with 440 volt electricity and lived, had crippled a young woman in a car accident years ago, had gone bankrupt twice, had seven daughters, none of whom would help in the sawmill, lived in Delmont— about ten miles north of South Dennis—and had brought his skiff, which he'd had for seven years, to the creek

26

because he'd lost his dockage on the Maurice River over a dispute with a Pole. And he knew Popeye, who didn't really own the dock where Jack kept his boat, but had known the old guy who used to own it who apparently had died, so Popeye gave him permission to use it. And that's not all he said. But it's all I can remember. Like I said, he was the most talkative person I had ever met.

The boat was named "Millie." That wasn't Jack's wife's name; it was the name the boat came with, he said, and he liked it better than his wife's name, which was Bert. When we got to the "Millie," it only took about three minutes for Jack to put the part in, then the engine roared to life. She had a nice healthy sound. He said let's take a shakedown cruise, so Freddy and I tied our boat to the same lonesome piling the "Millie" was tied to. Jack had been on his way out when the engine quit, but now he said it was too late to tend to his nets, so this was just a check-out ride.

The boat was faster than we expected. Jack tended to look bad tempered all the time, but I could see a slight twinkle in his eyes when he saw how much fun we boys were having. I thought if I never accomplish anything else in my life, having a boat like that of my own would be enough. Jack was quiet at first, tilting his head a bit as he listened to the motor. But as we blasted past Mosquito Point, which I'd never seen from the water before, and on out into the bay, his jaw began to loosen up again. He had to shout a little because of the engine noise, but he kept right at it once he started. He said that running a boat was like flying an airplane—not perfectly steady under you, and steering by "the seat of your pants."

"A plane's prob'ly more fun," he said, "but a boat's more relaxin'. You can kill yourself a lot quicker in a plane, I guess that's why. 'Course, you can kill yourself just as dead in boat, and usually in a slower, more agonizing way."

I knew where this was leading. I couldn't hear every word because of the engine noise, but I got most of it. He told us about two guys who got tangled in their gill net (which is a long net you stretch between poles or anchors out in the bay and fish get their gills tangled up in them) and drowned, how they were found a week later, and what they looked like. And he told about a guy he knew who crashed a crop duster and how he came all apart with the plane. "His hands was two-hundred foot apart, which gives you an idea what the rest of him looked like..." He liked to tell stories, the gruesomer the better. He told about car wrecks he'd seen and been in, sawmill accidents, and fatal fires. He started the Delmont Fire Co. in 1936. When he was talking about arson and how to detect it, I got an idea. Maybe he could help us with the Butterfly Leaming investigation. But it was hard to get the subject going, because Jack was a lot better at talking than listening. He would try to pay attention, but he would cut me off as soon as I stopped for breath. And I have to admit, he was funner to listen to than me. Everything I said reminded him of another story. After a while the bits and pieces of what I said must have settled in, like a delayed reaction, and he began to show a little interest. He'd heard about the fire, of course, and I knew it was right up his alley, with the burned corpse and all. He said if we were willing to work on it, he'd help us out with his "years of experience and know how" as he put it. He said he knew how easily the county detectives got discouraged investigating cases if they weren't real easy to solve. I was surprised that he didn't offer any answers right away, but he said he needed more facts. We said we'd get more and get back ahold of him.

𝔽 𝔽 𝔽

My dad didn't take it real good when I told him Freddy and I had been on a ride up the creek with old Jack Pugh. Of course, I didn't mention that we had rescued Jack, or I would have given away the fact that we had been out in the old, rotten garvey. I was kind of nervous dad would run into Jack somewhere and Jack would tell him about it.

"Anything goes wrong up at the creek now, boy, and that old man will pin it on you. I'm surprised the miserable old cuss even took you, considering his temperament. I've never seen a man get more stuff stolen from him—tools, batteries, material, equipment—it got so he couldn't leave a plane out at Woodbine Airport. And with his popularity, he'll get robbed again, or his boat sunk. You know how he lost his front teeth? He wouldn't give Bill Hickey his pay, so Bill hit him with a two-by-four. Don't you know Jack took that two-by-four off Bill, who was a good twenty years younger, and beat him over the head till he was out cold, Jack spittin' blood and teeth the whole time. Some people say he's colorful, but I've done business with him. He ain't colorful. He's mean, with the foulest mouth I ever heard when he gets mad. He's not what I'd call the 'good influence type.'"

I didn't say anything 'cause when dad gets going like that, it's best to just ride it out. I got lucky. He got distracted with a phone call. I sat there looking patient and interested a while as he talked, then casually slipped away. I got on my bike and started riding. My mind runs along and gets a lot of thinking done when I ride my bike. The trouble was I found myself heading for the creek. It's like there's a magnet pulling me that way. It wasn't where I had set out for. I hadn't set out for anywhere in particular. But I should have know that's where I'd end up. Between my dad's lecture, the secret boat, and Billy C., I wasn't feeling too brash. So I decided to stash my bike in the bushes that start just before the landing, and slip in the back way so nobody'd notice me. I figured I'd case the place, and if there was anybody there I didn't want to see or be seen by, I'd sneak back out the way I came and jump on my bike, which was very fast.

CHAPTER FOUR

Billy C.

Everything was O.K., no sign of life, so I relaxed, till I came out to where the boat was. There, clamped right to the transom, was a new-looking, 9.9 hp. Evinrude motor! Under the seat was a six gallon gas tank. For a minute I hoped Freddy's dad had put it there, but I knew better. My stomach got queasy. As much as I liked outboards, this one was contaminated—and it contaminated the boat. I knew Billy C. had put it there. I would have unclamped it and thrown it in the creek, but I was afraid Billy C. would find out. Now Billy C. and I were connected. And I didn't know what to do. I had that feeling you get on the first day of school when you find out you got Miss Meacham, the tough teacher, instead of Mrs. Locklear, the easy one. Only this was much worse, because my heart was pumping that nasty tingle of fear through my veins. I wanted to just leave and pretend it wasn't my boat. But Billy C. knew it was. I was in his thoughts, in his plans. Pictures of him pounding on Butterfly, breaking into Pedrick's store, stealing cars, stealing outboards, all went through my head. I couldn't call the cops. How could I prove he stole it? And Billy would find out for sure.

"Joe!"

My heart jumped right out of my throat. It was Billy C. Why was I so stupid not to stay hidden?

"I seen you jump. You wouldn't make a very good Indian if I can sneak up on you with my limp. How do you like your new outboard?"

"D-did you bring that, Bill?" Was my voice shaking? I was trying to seem casual, but I doubted it was working.

"Yeah, I bought it for you."

"That's alright, Bill. No thanks."

"It's yours, man. Don't worry about it."

"I-ah-I can't afford, ah, pay for it."

"Don't worry about it. Let's go for a ride."

"I-I can't, Bill."

"The hell you can't, boy. I get you a stinkin' motor, the least you can do is take me for a ride."

"I don't know how to work it, Bill." By now I was really panicking. If I got in the boat, who knows what he'd do. If I didn't, he might really get mad—then what? But I had to do something.

"Just a short one, Bill. O.K.?"

Billy squeezed the bulb on the gas line, saying, "Pump it till it's hard—you know how to do that—put the throttle on 'start,' give her a little choke and pull the cord." The engine sputtered to life in a cloud of blue smoke. Billy clunked it into reverse and swung the boat around.

"Here, you tak'er, Joe. I'll set back and smoke a number." Great, I thought, now he's smoking pot.

"Give'er some gas, boy. I'll bail."

The boat was fairly dry so I guessed Billy C. had bailed it out before I got there, probably when he brought the motor. I wondered how he got it there, but I didn't ask. The tide was three-quarters full and coming in, and underneath the fear and fright I also felt a kind of pleasure when the boat lunged ahead. It just about planed with the outboard. Too bad Billy C. had brought it. After we'd been going six or eight minutes, Billy said, "pull up to this island."

Now I got a new wave of fear. This would be a good place to bury me, and nobody'd find me for years. Old Claude Abrams had told my dad and me about the tow path that ran most of the length of the creek along the North, or Dennisville, shore. Men and sometimes mules would pull the big ships—"ships of hundreds of tons" as the sign out on Route 47 said—from the landing out to deeper water. The "islands" weren't really islands, but pieces of hard ground along the bank surrounded on the other three sides with marshes or littler creeks, and which had kind of filled in and grown cedar trees and stuff. And you could only get to them by boat. There are about five or six of them along the creek where the tow path used to be, and this was about the biggest one, with a big pin oak tree that had an open grassy area under it. I never thought, in all the times I pictured it—I'd only ever seen it from a great distance since Freddy and I had never been this far up the creek, outside of our trip with Jack—that it might be a place where I'd be marooned, or worse.

"Hey, we better tie'er to something. Here—tie'er to this cedar tree, Joe. You daydreaming or something? We should'a brought some beer. I didn't buy that motor, Joe. But don't tell nobody. I took it from Pineview campground. Some Philly idiot. He won't miss it."

"I don't want it, Billy."

"Don't be a sissy, boy. You didn't steal it. Ignore the Philly people. You wanna see my stash?"

This was bad. I was getting sucked in over my head. Things can sure get cruddy fast. My guts were churning again. Wouldn't it be nice if all you had to worry about was school starting and how soon is recess and not getting too much homework? Stuff that had always seemed bad seemed like luxuries now. I felt almost like I was watching what was going on, like in a dream.

"Look at this stuff, Joe. I brought it out on your boat. Who's that old fossil with the fishing boat? I seen him going out. Might be about time he found himself another place to tie up."

There was a metal box—not exactly a safe, more like a small filing cabinet. It was painted the same green they use in schools. It was in the bushes on the far side of the island. It was near what must have at one time been either an outhouse or a duckblind. There were some mattresses near it. Maybe Billy C. had slept out here. They were musty, like they'd been rained on. When he opened the box, I could see plastic bags of pot in it. A lot, it looked like. And there were coffee cans with lids on with stuff in them that I couldn't see what it was. And there were papers, maybe documents, underneath, which I couldn't make out, whether they were important or just lining the box. On T.V., this is usually when the criminal kills you, after he's told you his secrets, only unlike T.V., there was no cop or private eye ready to jump out and save me. He hadn't shown me everything in the box, of course, but he did show me the pot.

"I killed a guy once," he said. "Raped a girl, too. Black, the one I killed was black. Nobody'll miss him. Cut his head off. He had it coming. So did the girl. Rich from Sea Isle. Snooty. Let me come over to her house. Kept acting like she liked me. Which she did. She was a big tease, though. Wouldn't put out. Took me out on her old man's boat skiing, but I can't swim, so I wasn't about to go skiing. So when we were out down some ditch behind Avalon, I ripped off her bikini and threw it overboard. Her towel, too. We rode around a bit. She started calling me names. So I run up another ditch, shut off the motor, smacked her in the head, pinned her down and let her have it. Now she was really mad. I rode around some more, and she got kind of quiet and just cried, which angered me. So I got off the boat over by Townsend's Inlet. She had to drive that boat home nekked. Told her if she ratted, I'd kill her. I'd like to seen her old man when she showed up. He never much liked me anyway."

This sounded like a lie, and that cheered me up a bit. A girl from Sea Isle taking Billy C. water skiing? Sure. She had to drive home naked but was scared to tell the cops because she was scared of Billy C. even thought he'd already raped her? And if he killed Butterfly, why did he tell me the black story?

"But that cow put the cops on me—well her old man did, soon as she got home," Billy said after a pause. "Come around and picked me up. Spent thirty-eight days in county jail. Couldn't make it stick, though, or maybe they figured she had it coming, just like I did. Her old man's a Italian. S'posed to be in the Mafia, like all the Italians claim. Ain't killed me yet, though. You scared, Joe? You don't look too good. I ain't gonna mess with you. Your old man's a friend of my old man. They worked together years ago, I think. Don't tell him about any of this, thought. He'd have the cops on me. Then I'd be on you. But that's alright. You won't tell him, will ya?"

I didn't want to know any of it. I wished I could just leave and put it out of my mind. The more he told me, the more I felt like a fly getting tied up in a spider web. Some of it must have been true, maybe all of it. He did seem to spend some time in jail, so he must have been doing something bad.

"How about we get going, Bill. I don't want my old man to come looking for me."

"He wouldn't find you out here, anyway. He don't even know you've got this boat, I bet. This is the last place anybody'd look. That's what's so good about it."

"He's a pain sometimes, though. You know that. I'd just as soon get going."

"Yeah, alright. You don't mind if I use your boat from time to time, do you?"

"Nah—go ahead. We'd better not let my dad find out though."

I had to say yes. What else could I do? I had hoped mentioning my dad would scare him a bit, but it didn't seem to. My mind was running all over the place. Everything ran together. I guess we got back and tied the boat up, but I don't really remember. I was home before I realized I'd gotten on my bike. Home sure looked comfortable when I got there. I felt like a young soldier coming home from war—or at least what I thought a young soldier might feel like. I had left the house innocent and happy, and came back sick with fear. I couldn't tell anybody at my house, either. In a way, I wanted to tell my dad right out and get it off my chest, but I knew he'd be so mad and disappointed in me. My mom wouldn't be as mad, but she'd be even more disappointed. And naturally she'd tell my dad. And I didn't want to drag my sister into it and burden her with such a secret and all the dreadful stories. She still lived in the nice world I had lived in before my ride with Billy C. And it all started with sneaking out in that garvey. Because at first I had lied (or at least hid the truth) about the boat, I now had to conceal everything else. It sure didn't seem worth it, but I was in too deep to change it. If only I hadn't got tied up with that stupid boat, which wasn't any good anyway....

CHAPTER FIVE

The Crabbers

The good part was that I got to tell Freddy. I was bursting to get hold of him, even as bad as I felt, which was as bad as I could ever remember. At first I was going to juice it up a little bit, like I knew him and his dad did with their stories, but I decided it was already juicy enough.

At the supper table my mom asked me what was wrong. How did she do that? She always knew when something was up. I could tell she didn't believe me when I said it was nothing, but there's no way she could have guessed how bad it was. I finally got loose after supper and went straight to Freddy's. He was in his living room, so I had to invent a reason to take him outside. He's kind of slow at getting hints. "I don't want to see the new tire on your bike—I'll look at it tomorrow." I think he was the only one in the room who didn't pick up on it.

When I got him outside and began to tell him the story, he tried to act cool at first, like it was no big deal. But it got to him fairly quick, and he started to get excited. First his eyes got a glint, then he started shooting questions at me. The more I told him, the better I felt. Freddy was very practical. He was for getting Billy C. put in jail without mentioning the outboard, so we'd have it free and clear. "All we need is another investigation, only this time, we've got to finish and have an airtight case," he said. "An anonymous tip ain't good enough. Billy C. could just deny it about the drugs and stuff, and say they ain't his if the cops find them. And we ain't even sure about the murder or the rape."

Fred wasn't real realistic, though. He thought we could just watch "Columbo" on T.V. and write down everything he does. I said Columbo always figures it out because the guys who write the stories know who the killer is before they decide how Columbo is going to solve it. He said yea, but they're based on real stories, which I don't know if they are. It was easy for Freddy to feel so relaxed about it, because he hadn't been on the boat with Billy C. feeling his guts churn like I had.

I decided to go along with his investigation plan, though. Even if it didn't work like he said, it wouldn't hurt to get more information while I decided what to do, as long as we laid low and didn't let Billy C. catch us.

                🏴   🏴   🏴

Freddy said he heard from Ronnie Winslow that Gloria Hunt and Sandy Spinelli sometimes go skinny dipping at a little pond along the railroad tracks on the way to the creek. So Freddy and I decided it might be better to walk along the tracks rather than take our bikes. We saw no sign of the girls as we passed the little pond, but the chance that we might have gave us a little lift. The tracks hit the creek about a quarter mile east of the Route 47 landing, the opposite direction from the bay. We had to go on an old muskrat trapper's path to get across the marshes, since there's no hard bank on the creek between the railroad tracks and Route 47. The path belonged to a guy named Icky Whilden, and we weren't really allowed on it. But it

40

would have been hard for him to catch us. It was grown up with reeds and cedar trees, which offered good protection, and anyway, Icky was eighty-three years old and not as fast as he'd once been. Icky stands for Ichabod, but Icky suits his personality better.

We brought along some candy bars and colas, so we were able to set up a pretty comfortable camp in the bushes with a clear shot of the boat and dock. We figured to lay low and keep our eyes open, and when Billy C. Showed up we would take notes of what he did. But we hadn't thought about how long it might be before he showed up. After about an hour we started getting impatient. We got kind of confident just from sitting there so long undisturbed, so we got up to take a walk and find a new and interesting hiding place. We shot out and over the bridge to the Dennisville shore, showing ourselves as briefly as possible. The Dennisville shore has a little road along it for a ways, which is lined with reeds, which are good cover, and since Billy C. had no business over there we felt relatively safe. This little road once went miles down the creek, part of the old tow path, but now it wasn't half a mile long. We walked up to the end where an old shack used to be. You could see our landing from it, but we decided it was too far. We were shuffling back towards the bridge when we heard a car door slam over by our dock. We looked through the reeds and saw a red VW bus parked at the landing. We stole down to where we were just opposite our dock and crouched in the reeds. We thought maybe it was a drug dealer come to meet Billy C. A tall, dark man in this thirties with a dark mustache and a boy about nine were getting crab traps out of the car. They put bait on three of them, then tossed them into the creek, tying the strings to our dock poles. They got out two lawn chairs and set them right on our rickety dock. These were interlopers, Freddy whispered, we must get rid of them. But the guy looked pretty big to chase, and I pointed out that it wasn't any more our dock than it was his. His brashness did get me, though. He set out a bushel basked to put the crabs in, which was kind of optimistic, and turned on a little portable radio. It was fun spying, even though we realized these two weren't exactly criminals. We could sort of hear them talking, but couldn't understand them, so I figured Freddy's whispering and fidgeting wouldn't give us away.

After a while our attention strayed off the crabbers and we started noticing things around the creek, things you usually overlook if you're not sitting still on the bank for an hour. We talked about the old bulkheads—how they were pegged together, and how the timbers were flat on the top and bottom. We looked at the hulk of a long ago sunk oyster schooner, which was now a permanent part of the other bank, and talked about the other hulks we had explored—one still had the cabin on it—about what life must have been like on an old time schooner, and whether women or girls were allowed to come along on long voyages. That got us on the subject of girls in general, and we speculated about what Sandy Spinelli and Gloria Hunt must look like naked—pretty good, we thought, especially Sandy—and about girls' breasts and stuff, and Freddy asked if I had ever actually touched one, which he hadn't. I said I had, which was stretching it a little. I had felt one of Eileen Oliver's once accidentally on purpose through her sweater during a football pile up. I was just

42

getting to the consistency—a bit like a water balloon, I was saying, when we heard raised voices from over where the crabbers were.

"...Doing...dock?"

Me and Fred stopped short. There was Billy C., confronting the crabber. He'd come out of nowhere again, just when our attention had drifted. We could only make out odd words, but you could tell Billy was giving him a hard time about being on "his" dock. They were standing about two feet apart, and the crabber was a lot taller than Billy C. The little boy was about eight feet behind the crabber. All of a sudden Billy C. threw down the jacket he'd been holding and put up his fists like an old time boxer, the palm side of his fists curling back towards him, and his left hand extended farther than his right. He looked kind of silly, and at first I thought the big guy wasn't in much danger, but even from across the creek you could see a killer look in Billy's eyes. I looked down quickly at Freddy, who had been squirming as usual, and when I looked back up I saw Billy punch the guy twice real quick in the nose with his left hand, making his head snap back. The guy put up his hands and looked real alarmed, and pawed at Billy C. as they circled each other. Right then I could see that the crabber was no fighter. Twice Billy C. flicked out his left hand, then, with his right hand, cracked him square in the chin. It didn't look like a tremendous punch from where we were, but the guy instantly collapsed, like somebody had just flipped a switch. I was surprised when the guy just laid flat on his back, perfectly still. Billy stood there looking at him for a minute, like you might look at a cat that's just been hit by a car, then glanced up for a scary second at the boy, who still stood like a statue where he'd been all along. Then he stooped down and picked up his jacket and walked briskly off towards Route 47.

Freddy and I stood up and looked at the man across the creek. He still laid there perfectly still. The little boy walked towards him slowly.

"We gotta get over there and help, Fred," I said. It seemed like we were just frozen.

"I know we do," Fred said. "But maybe we better wait till Billy's good and gone."

"Well, we'll stay low along this road and scout as we go, but we can't waste any time."

We ran along in a crouch so we'd stay hid by the reeds till we got to the bridge, then just busted out and ran over to the guy. The little boy was on his haunches looking down at his dad, kind of in a daze. My guts were already a little loose from what happened, and there wasn't any improvement when I saw the guy up close. His nose was swollen and bluish in the middle, he had a cut on his forehead, and thick blood was oozing from behind his head, soaking the ground and the small slab of concrete his head was on. Of all the places to fall, he had hit this slab somebody had put there to shore up the bank. His eyes were slightly open, and his skin was turning greyish-blue. I thought maybe he was dead—he looked it. Freddy stood a few feet behind me.

"Touch him, Joe. See if he's breathing."

"Run over to Popeye's and call the cops, Fred."

"Not me. You go. I'll watch the kid. Billy might be over there."

Old Popeye still lived in the back of the clam stand, which was across the street and over on the Dennisville side. He hadn't sold any clams for years, and the place looked deserted, but he was back there. Billy C. probably wouldn't bother him since the old man always carried a .32 caliber revolver in his back pocket. He was real unfriendly and had a lot of cats. I was at his place once with my dad, who Popeye had called to give an estimate for raising up his house. He had a pile of sand in the store part of the building, which the cats used instead of a litter box. The cats had sores on their eyes and were mangy. And my eyes watered from the smell. Popeye's skin was real greasy, and his clothes looked like he'd been wearing them for a year. It seemed like I was outside myself watching what was going on as I knocked on his door, remembering my last visit. I would never do this normally, but it was like I was on automatic pilot. Popeye just looked bored and didn't say anything when I told him what had happened, and after staring at me for a couple of long seconds, pointed to the phone on the wall.

"The cops' number's right here," he said, pointing with a long, filthy fingernail. "911." He looked even more disgusting than I'd remembered him. As he walked away, I saw the pistol with electrical tape on the handle sticking out of his back pocket. "You know what to tell 'em, boy; it ain't my concern."

The dispatcher was a lady, and she asked me to describe the attacker.

"Shortish, stocky, flannel shirt..."

"Black?"

"No, white. Army pants." I gave her the location, and thankfully, she never asked my name. I tore back across the street. I thought maybe Popeye didn't believe me—it sure didn't worry him too much. But if he hadn't believed me, he probably wouldn't have let me use the phone. He made me feel like I must have been making it up, and I wish I had, but it was real enough. When I got back the guy was still motionless. The boy was still on his haunches, with little tears on his face. He looked more scared than dazed now. Fred still stood a little ways back. He said, "I'm pretty sure he's breathing. His chest heaved a couple times. Not real regular, though. Maybe we ought to cover him with something."

"Yeah. Let's look in his van."

We found an old blanket on the back seat that was covered with dog hairs. It reminded me of Popeye—the stink from his house was still in my nose and mouth. We took the blanket from the car and spread it over the guy.

"Maybe we oughtta get outta here," I said. "There's no more we can do."

"Yeah."

"But what about the boy? It ain't right to leave him, I guess. We're in this deep, we better stay."

"Maybe we oughtta say we didn't see it happen, Joe."

"I kinda already said I did. At least I described Billy to the lady. I didn't say who I was, though."

"Then she don't have to know it was you."

"What's your name?" I asked the boy.

"T-Tony. Like my dad. He's big Tony."

My heart went up in my throat. All this time I'd been thinking of Freddy and me more than this man and his little boy. When he said his name, it really hit home. This was a real person, and somebody's father. Sure, I'd felt bad. And I was trying to help. But I was also thinking about my own neck, too. What if this was my dad? I wanted to do something, but was scared of getting involved. My heart was really pounding, even after I caught my breath from running, and I realized I was starting to panic. So was Freddy, I guess. Maybe that's why we were worrying about ourselves so much.

"What were they fighting about?" I asked the boy.

"The guy said it was his dock, and we had to leave," Tony, Jr. said in a tiny voice. "My dad said, 'You don't look like you own any dock to me.' Then the guy said my dad could use it if he paid $5.00. My dad said no, and they started fighting. I thought my dad could take him. You think he's dead? He hasn't moved yet."

"I don't think so. Let me check his pulse."

"You check in the neck," Tony, Jr. said.

My hands were shaking. I felt cold. Tony's neck felt warm.

"I feel it," I said. I didn't really, but I wanted to make little Tony feel better. I still had my hand on his neck when I did feel something. "Yeah," I said. "There it is," trying to act calm.

I knew the state cops had to come from Port Norris, which is more than twenty-five miles away, unless they had a cruiser nearby. The ambulance only had to come from Dennisville, though, and it was there pretty quick. I hadn't even said anything about an ambulance when I called—I asked her to send a cop, though naturally an ambulance was more important.

The ambulance guys were real cool and business-like. One was Bill Post, a friend of my dad's. They put Tony on a stretcher and took his blood pressure and were talking on the radio. As they whisked him into the ambulance, Ed Post said to Tony, Jr., "You ride with us. This your Dad? I guess you called it in, huh, Joe?" He didn't seem to care about the crime aspect of it. He just gave me a little wave as he closed the back door, and they took off. We figured this was a good time to take off, too, before the cops arrived.

"Billy C. is rotten," I said, after we'd walked a ways. "Before I thought he was bad. All that talk scared me, but it was just talk. This is real bad. I feel like puking."

"I felt like that ever since it happened," Freddy said. "I didn't want to say it. He could have killed Butterfly. I believe it now. That guy didn't want to fight him. He just didn't want to back down. He never even threw a punch, just kind of flailed at him. I guess he never thought Billy would hit him like that. When Billy really popped him in the nose he got pretty scared, I think. Billy knew it. That's why he knocked him out. It's a good thing you didn't look too scared when you were out on that island with him. I think it brings out the killer in him."

"Yeah, he'd be scared of my Dad, too. Of course, he ain't too scared by the cops or that Mafia guy over Sea Isle, if that story's true, which it might be. Maybe we oughtta find that girl and ask her. We gotta do something.

"What're we gonna do, ask every girl in Sea Isle with an Italian name, which is most of them, 'You ever have any trouble with Billy C. Tobin? You wanna tell me and my fourteen year old friend about it?' No, Joe, we have to tell our dads. But not our moms. They'd get too scared."

"You think our dads wouldn't tell our moms, Fredrick? We wouldn't be allowed out of the house till we were twenty. Then when we were, Billy C. would kill us. Maybe if we just talk about the fight, not Butterfly or the drugs or our boat."

"Let's see if it's in the paper tomorrow and decide then," Freddy said, which wasn't a bad idea.

We stopped at Pedrick's and got a couple of sixteen ounce R.C. Colas, and went into the graveyard to relax.

We went to the Leaming family plot, which is a group of five or six graves surrounded by a cast iron fence and big boxwood hedges. It's nice and hollow and private inside. We leaned on James and Abigail Leaming's stones, which are gently slanted and make a nice back rest.

"Let's hold our mud a day or two," I said, after reflecting a while. "It can't hurt. It won't do Tony any good if we tell anyway. If he needs evidence later, we'll testify. In the meantime, we don't want Billy C. catching wind of what we know. Let's stay clear of the creek a while, too. Maybe Billy'll get picked up, and we'll be out of danger. I just hope Ed Post don't say anything to the cops about us being there. I think maybe ambulance drivers got immunity, like priests and doctors. Like I say, maybe Billy'll get picked up in the meantime, and we'll be out of danger."

At the dinner table that night I had a hard time eating, which is unusual. I kept picturing Tony—not on purpose, he was just always there—and his little, scared son. I saw big Tony's face, perfectly still, eyes slightly open, just some of the white part showing. I wondered how he was. I thought how sometimes boxers get knocked cold for several minutes. But then they don't hit concrete, just taut canvas. It didn't look like much of a punch, short and kind of choppy. And Billy was even leaning back a little. Maybe Billy's really strong, I thought. Or maybe by chance he hit him just right, or Tony has a glass jaw. But Tony never moved once he fell, even after the ambulance guys worked on him. One piece of concrete at the whole landing and that's where he had to fall. I wished I could get Tony's face out of my head. But it was there, and when it wasn't, there was little Tony's. And Billy C., with that hard-eyed look.

"You alright,son?" my dad asked. "You look like you just ate a bar of Ivory soap."

"I'm O.K. My stomach's a little queasy, though."

"Too many Tastykakes," my mom said. "You and Freddy go over to Pedrick's entirely too much. You'll rot your teeth out with that junk."

"Ease up, Ma," my dad cut in. "He's already looking peaked. Your mom's right, though. You'll end up looking like old lady Hughes if you eat too much of that trash. Did you know they're puttin' her in the *Guinness Book of Records* for most wrinkles? Hey, we're movin' a big rancher over Sea Isle tomorrow. Just eight blocks. You want to drive her?"

"Yeah, sure," I said.

I thought about how strong my dad was. "That Joe Bass is a powerful man" everyone says. My dad says they say that because they think he moves the houses by hand instead of using jacks. I pictured my dad getting hit flush in the chin, his head bouncing as it hit the ground. I wondered if that could happen. Of course my dad could punch—not like Tony. People said he'd done it when he was young more than once. I thought about the time my dad's old boss got crushed by a house when a jack shifted. I always thought of him as "the man who got crushed"—I'd never even seen him. Now I realized it had been a real person my dad knew. It must have been real grisly. My dad and some other guys tried to jack the house back up. The guy was still talking for a while, but finally died. Yet my dad had cheered up since then—I wondered how. I wondered if I could.

CHAPTER SIX

Moving A House

My dad woke me about six o'clock. I had forgotten I'd said I would go to work with him that day. It was always fun to go in with him because he'd take me out to breakfast over at Marge's where he was a pretty big shot. They called him "Big Joe," and of course they always had to know why "little Joe" was with him today. "Brought the big guns out today, huh, Joe?" They were endlessly interested in what job dad was working on, and whether he was a sliding a house off a lot, or spinning one, or going down the road, or whatever.

His two workers were Roy Thompson, a black guy about sixty years old who used to be a crane operator and a fisherman, and Larson Cole, a heavyset, red-faced guy who used to be captain of a clam boat until it sank. Those two were in the power truck, and they met us at the job. Me and dad rode over in his single axle Mack tractor, which I was going to drive when we pulled the house. It had a duplex transmission—two gearshifts, and ten possible gears —but I would only have to stay in low because we were just going ten blocks. The house was on a low lot, and had to be winched off with the power truck. When dad needed an extra pair of hands he always stuck me in the truck pulling the house, because that is the one person who always stays put and therefore is always safe. He used to say it wouldn't put my mom in a very good mood if he brought me home rolled up like a piece of carpet after a truck ran over me or a house fell on me. Let the old guys crawl under the house or hop in and out of the winch truck.

Dad backed the Mack under the bolster that held the I-beams together that went under the house. He backed up till the fifth wheel clunked in to the kingpin under the bolster. Once the truck was hooked up, I climbed over to the driver's seat and waited. I watched as Roy positioned the big power truck in front of me and a little to the left, and began paying out cable from the winch. Larson pulled it back as it came off the drum till it was far enough to reach the bolster, then he hooked it up. All the while my dad was putting up cones and directing traffic. He had a hand-held VHF, and I had the VHF in the Mack turned on so he could make funny comments to me when people shook their fists at him for having the road blocked off. When Roy was ready, my dad gave him the word to start taking in cable. When the house started moving ahead just a little bit he told me to put the truck in low, then let out the clutch. The truck started hopping and he said "push it in" real quick. "Wait till you're moving." He watched the left side and Larson watched the right. It was real slow but steady, and in about three minutes I was almost out on the road. Then all of a sudden my dad said "let her rip" and me and Roy both dumped our clutches and poured on the gas. Smoke was pouring out of Roy's stack, and I really had to saw on the wheel to follow him around. Once you get moving off a soft lot, you can't stop or you'll get stuck and sink. The "China Syndrome" is what they call it. It's exciting because both trucks are straining, and the cable's straining, and you have this great big house behind you gently rocking as it climbs the crown of the road and straightens out. It looks so strange to see a house moving like that, with the shutters still one and the furniture all in place. It gives me a thrill every time. And once you get on the street, everything seems so secure and stable, you just putt along, a guy with a flag on either side directing you if you get too close to parked cars or telephone poles. They unhooked Roy's cable and wound it up so he could ride a little farther ahead with his lights flashing. Since a house usually takes up both lanes and part of the shoulder, people have to make a complete detour, and believe it or not, they don't always notice the house—I guess they're not used to seeing one on the street and their brains don't register. Sometimes my dad gets a police escort, but since we were just going ten blocks on a weekday they left it up to us. When we got to the new lot, I went around to the back and pulled the house forward right over the new foundation, which had the ends left off so you could drive over it. It was a lot easier than backing on, and my dad hopped in and sawed up and back a couple of times till it was just right and shut off the engine.

Roy hollered "break time" and pulled out his thermos as we got down from the truck. We sat around on some stacks of cribbing and congratulated ourselves on doing such a good job, and it wasn't long until the conversation got around to past triumphs in housemoving, which inevitably reminded Larson of his clamming days.

"When we was clammin'" he would always start out. This time it reminded him of the cold January day when his one hundred and five foot clam boat sank off Cape May. As many times as I'd ever heard him tell clamming stories,

I hadn't ever heard him tell this one. I knew the story from other people, but I figured it was something he didn't want to talk about.

"It was back in '75, colder'n hell. She was a big, old schooner, with the sails took off, and a big Alco diesel. Eleven foot draft. She could take just about any sea there was, gen'rly, and never leaked a drop as long as you didn't tighten down on the stays. It was cold, though, like I say, and ice was beginning to build up. We was having a hard time seeing out of the cabin. We had a hold full of clams, and a deckload of quahogs we'd scooped up just outside Townsend's Inlet. We were only about five mile off, heading for Cold Spring Inlet, when we went over a little shoal, where the sea was near ten to fifteen foot. Lenny Justis was at the wheel, and he got sort of shook up and tried to steer off the shoal, which was thirty foot deep—no danger of grounding. He should'a pulled right though it. But instead, he steered off to port and we took three great crashing seas right sideways. She came off the first one O.K., though you could'a stood on the side of the cabin when it hit, and she hadn't righted properly when the second one hit. I reckon the load of clams in the hull shifted. The ones on top were pretty much frozen in place, but made the ship top heavy. The second wave pushed us further over to starboard so that we was just about sideways, all banged up against the wall of the cabin, when the third one hit. The engine had quit—starved for fuel, I guess—after that second one hit, and it was a few long seconds of what seemed like silence—even though the seas roared and the winds whistled—before that third one slammed us. We knew it was coming, of course, waves always come in

57

groups of three. At least me and Big Bill Moncrief knew it—he was the other man aboard. But I don't think Lenny Justis knew it. It was his third or fourth trip out. He was twenty-five, and now I'm sorry I had him steering the boat. Me and Big Bill was trying to get the radio to work, and I just said steer for 120 on the compass. He'd done it before. He never even knew he caused the wreck. He didn't live to find out. We busted out of the cabin O.K., and by a miracle, when we popped to the surface, we found a piece of the life raft that had busted loose from the cabin, and we all three grabbed it. We was very fortunate the Mabel Kim was less than a mile behind us. They seen what happened and come right over to try and pull us out. I seen her coming and said "Hang on, boys, we're gonna be alright." Lenny couldn't hold out, though. Before the boat got to us, he got a real sleepy look on his face and just slid down into the sea. See, he was just thin as a rail, thin and muscular, so he didn't have any insulation. Me and Bill was both about thirty to forty pounds overweight, and that's what saved us.

The worst thing was, somebody had to tell Justis's wife. I tried to get Bill to do it, but he said "you're the captain." So I drove over that afternoon after spending about three hours in the hospital, and there was his wife, Jeanne. I'd never even met her before. She was out in the yard, baby in her arms and toddler by the hand. 'You the widow Justis?' I asked. 'I'm Jeanne Justis,' she said kinda starchy, 'but I'm not a widow.' 'The hell you ain't,' I said."

58

And with that, everybody roared, except me. I was horrified.

"Short and sweet," Roy said, still chuckling.

"No bull," Larson said.

After that we put some tools away and unhitched the tractor, then we headed home. I knew my dad felt bad about the way I reacted to Larson's story. "That didn't really happen—you knew that didn't you? I mean he didn't really tell Mrs. Justis that way. They did sink, of course. The rest of it's true. But telling young Justis's wife about it has always bugged Larson. He has about five versions of how he told her, each one more ridiculous than the last."

It was a lot like Jack's stories, but even realer, in a way. I was still feeling kind of glum, though. It took some of the appeal away from commercial fishing, which had always been my ambition.

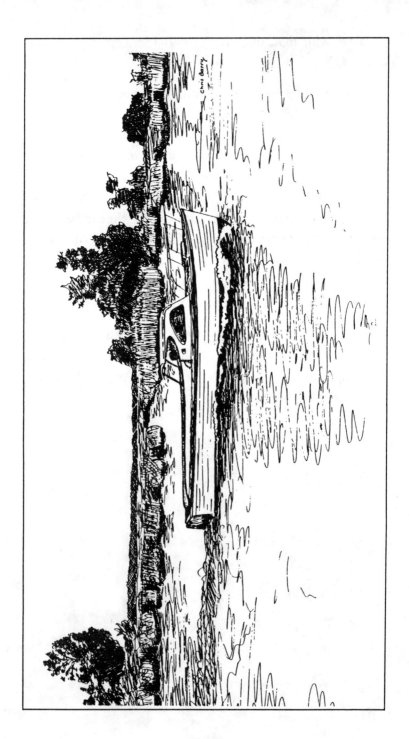

CHAPTER SEVEN

The Fishing Trip

After a few days of scanning the obituaries for a "Tony, Sr." survived by a "Tony, Jr.", and having nothing turn up, I started to feel a little better.

It was a while before Freddy and I went to the creek again, and when we did, we sneaked up through the bushes only to find the boat was gone. We figured Billy was out in it, and so we set up camp for a while. It was easier to listen for a boat motor than for Billy slinking up on foot, so we were more relaxed than we might have been otherwise. After a while we investigated the bank, and saw how our foot prints looked, and noticed that there weren't any fresh ones besides ours. Then we saw that all the ropes were gone. And all the scraps of lumber we kept there. It had rained three days ago, and we hadn't been there since before then. It didn't look like anybody else had either. So that creep had stolen our boat! Now we were mad. When it dawned on us that Billy C. had stolen *our* boat, and even our ropes and stuff, it seemed worse than killing Butterfly, which of course we weren't sure he did. But this we were sure of, and it made the other crimes seem a lot more likely. I remembered the threats he made about old Jack Pugh, back when he and I were on the island, and I told Freddy we ought to tell the old man. Something made me think that he might be the guy to talk to about this whole thing anyway. My dad would get so mad at Freddy and me, it wouldn't be worth it if we told him.

And Freddy's dad would blab the whole thing to everybody, including my dad, but not do anything about it himself. And of course our moms would have a fit and tell our dads. That wouldn't be any help. And as I've said, I wouldn't want to drag my older sister into it. But we had to tell somebody. We had brought the subject up to Jack Pugh, but that was before we were so involved ourselves. Now it was even worse for us. We decided we'd better talk to him.

When we were snooping around his boat and didn't need any help, the old man had showed up and cussed us up one side and down the other. Now that we did need him, wouldn't you know he wasn't around. It took two days to catch up with him, which seemed like a year, because once we made up our minds to tell him we were fit to bust with the information. Freddy said he couldn't get to sleep and had almost told his mom a couple of times accidentally. When we finally saw old Jack, he was getting ready to take his boat out and didn't seem very glad to see us. We helped him put some plastic barrels in his boat, and that cheered him up some. "Somebody's gonna mess with your boat, and maybe you," I said, but he didn't seem very scared or impressed.

"How about if we go along and help you?" Freddy asked. He said, "No, you'll be in the way." Even though I was scared my dad would find out if we went out with him again, I was about to bust with the story.

"We need your help. We have nobody else to turn to." My dad says if you really want or need something, to go to a man and admit you need his help, and he won't turn you down. You better want it pretty bad, he says, to humble yourself like that, but it usually works.

"I ain't much for helping snot-nosed kids who get themselves into jams, but I did say I owe you one, if memory serves, so hop aboard and tell me yer sad tale."

We pushed off, and as we idled past the other docks Freddy and I took turns, with me doing most of the talking, telling the whole thing. I started with the fight at the dock, and Freddy told about the boat being missing. Unlike the last time, Jack was very quiet and hardly seemed to be paying attention but did nod once in a while as he looked straight ahead. We had to talk louder when he speeded the boat up after the second bend, but his expression never changed. I told him about Billy and the outboard, and the stash on the island, and when I said that he made a funny face: he sucked in his chin, and made his eyes look shocked and said "the hell you say," and slowed the boat right down to an idle. "Which island? You mean we got real evidence?"

"We're almost to it, I think. Next bend," I said.

We pulled up to the island and Freddy jumped off when we stopped in front of it. Jack threw him a piece of line, which he tied to the same handy cedar tree me and Billy C. had used, and Jack tied it to a cleat in the gunwale. Jack surprised me by jumping right over the soft edge to the hard grassy part of the bank. He was pretty nimble for an old guy.

"You ain't kidding me, are you boys? I got better things to do with my time than chase wild geese."

We swore it was the truth, and he seemed satisfied. He looked around very carefully, signaling for us not to crowd him. It was only then that I noticed the stuff was gone. He would stop every once in a while and stare at something with an eagle-eyed squint. Then he stopped and leaned his elbow on a branch of the oak tree, and kind of covered his mouth with his hand. And he stood perfectly still for a couple of minutes. Then he pulled his hand away and snapped back to life.

"Somebody's been here. And he's up to something. On that point you're correct. But of course he's moved camp. Either he doesn't trust you, or he's afraid somebody else is onto him. I seen somebody in a boat up around here, but shot down a sluice 'fore I could get much of a look at him. Probably just one guy. Nossir, he mustn't learn we're in cahoots. That would spook him worse. We've got to find him right quick before he burrows in any deeper. We got plenty of tide, which naturally is why I chose this time to tend my nets, so maybe we ought to do a little exploring and let the fish in the nets drown a little longer."

We got back in the boat and roared to Sluice Creek branch, barreling right on down to the Route 47 bridge, which is about three miles from our landing. Sluice Creek is one of the dozens of branches of the creek, and the biggest, and it was fun going up in the big boat. Jack was strictly business, though, and we roared on back out when nothing of interest caught his eye. Next we went up another, smaller sluice, and had to back out when we started churning mud. Then up Roaring Ditch and West Creek, two big branches out toward the bay. Then on out into the bay, and into East Creek and then Goshen Creek a little ways.

There were no signs of life, or stashes, but Jack said they'd be hard to find anyway because his boat was so big and Billy C. could have gone a lot farther up the little creeks than we could. He said the boat and the stash might or might not both be in the same place, depending on how smart or enterprising Billy C. was.

"Well, I did come out here to go fishing, boys," Jack said after a bit. "Our investigation ain't turned up nothin' yet, but give me a little time to think and I might come up with something. And there ain't nothin' quite like hard work to get a brain a-cookin'. Let's go lift a couple of gillnets and see what happens."

We weren't very far out in the bay when we got to the first net. Jack idled down, then stopped alongside a float made from a plastic Clorox bottle. Gillnets are anchored at each end, and have a float, or "buoy over each anchor. Jack's nets looked to be about three-hundred feet long. The nets have little floats all along the top and weights along the bottom so they hang in the water like a huge volleyball net. They have real fine line, but a large mesh, and the fish get part way through the mesh, then foul their gills on it if they're of the right size. Jack hoisted this first net up over the right hand (or starboard) side and stuck a short length of pipe into a rod holder on the gunwale up near the cabin to hold in on board. Then he slid more of the net on and stuck another pipe toward the back so that about twelve feet of net was in the boat with the rest of it trailing off the front and back. Then he stuck a tiller arm onto a steering rod that came up alongside the engine box, went up and clunked the boat in gear so that we were idling slowly ahead and steering for the far buoy. As we rolled along, Jack pulled the fish out of the nets and threw them into boxes according to what kind they were—mostly weakies, with some bunker and a few bluefish. I was fascinated watching the operation, and it was exciting to see what fish came up as we advanced. Once he pulled a drowned terrapin out of the net and threw it overboard. When we got to the end of the net, he pulled the pipes out and the net slid overboard and was gone. We went up into the cabin to cruise to the next net. The VHF radio was on, and Jack looked up at it real sharp when a voice he must have recognized came on through the static. "You out there, Pugh? I might have to head home to mama. Ripped by blue jeans clear up to my tailbone." It sounded like a strange thing to call someone on the radio about, but Jack said it meant he was "up to his tail in bluefish."

"We have to use a code so that every Tom, Dick and Devil with a Boston Whaler don't instantly converge on the place. Bluejeans is bluefish. Ripped means down at the Rips, off Cape May. If you boys don't have any pressing appointments, I vote we head down there and pick up a couple dollars worth. Ain't more'n a half an hour from where we are. They oughta keep biting that long. Take the wheel, Bass. Steer for 170 on the compass, and always keep the land to your left. Chance, me'n you are gonna dress up some rigs real quick. Bluefish ain't worth a million bucks apiece, but if you fill a few boxes you can always make out."

I was in an awful sweat trying to keep the boat on the numbers. I was sawing the wheel back and forth, and just as I got the heading going the right way, it would shoot on past the heading line and I'd have to work like crazy to get it back. When I had watched Jack driving, he moved the wheel quite gently and only occasionally glanced at the compass, so I had assumed it was real easy.

"We're gonna put a hundred mile on the boat before we get to Cape May the way you're going, son," Jack said. "Let's try a lighter touch," he added as he took the wheel. "Don't try to rassle her through the water. Aim for somethin' straight ahead, out on the horizon. Don't try to steer the compass. Steer the whole boat. Don't steer every time a wave hits. You gotta feel what direction you're going by the seat of your pants. The compass is just to tell you if you're doin' it right. If it stays a little to the left or the right of the numbers for a little bit don't lose any sleep over it. Just head the boat *gener'ly* in the right direction, and pretty soon you can keep 'er straight without hardly even trying'."

The whole time he was talking the number didn't vary left or right any more than one one-hundredth of an inch. And he had his hand on the wheel so casually you wouldn't have thought he was even paying attention.

"Once you got that feel, you can steer anything on the water. Not everybody's got the knack for it, but I got a hunch you can pick it up. Once you got that figured out I might have time to teach you how to navigate by dead reckoning."

I got a boost of confidence by that little compliment and set out to master this steering by the compass. I hoped Freddy wasn't offended that I was singled out for this honor, but he wasn't the nautical know-it-all that I was, so I figured he wouldn't be.

"If I steer for that dot up on the horizon, how do I know it's not a moving boat?" I asked.

"Steer for it and see if your compass is slowly gaining one way or the other. Don't rely too heavy on any one thing."

Jack wasn't smiling or acting jolly, but this was as upbeat as I'd ever seen him. I had a gnawing discomfort in my gut as I thought about my parents not knowing where I was, but I was doing what I had always dreamed of, and it was hard to feel bad for long. As I was concentrating on steering, my mind went over the idea of Jack helping us and all that might be involved, and I thought the friendlier we all got during this fishing trip the more seriously he'd take the investigation. That cheered me up about being out here without permission, because it gave the trip more of a purpose than just fun for Freddy and me.

When we got down to the "Rips" we saw a bunch of birds working, and Jack said, "that's them." He idled the boat down and showed us how to land the fish and knock them off on the "de-hooker" and into the box. It was a real frenzy on the boat and just about as much fun as I'd ever had. Sometimes all three of us would be hauling fish in at the same time. They were big—eight to ten pounders

—and put up a mighty struggle. Sometimes the lines would get tangled, but Jack would get them clear real quick or pull out another one. The action slowed down after about twenty minutes, but in that time we had filled two one-hundred pound boxes, and there were fish loose on the deck.

"Watch yer hands an' feet, boys. Them bluefish'll chop 'em like a meat grinder." We went along for about another half an hour, getting an occasional hit, but the fish must have lost their appetite. The birds had mostly drifted off, too, I now noticed.

"Let's go cash in our chips." Jack said. "That's Cape May right over there. Bass, take the wheel and steer for them jetties." We steamed towards the jetties and into the Cape May canal, right behind the ferries. When we got into the canal there was a lot of boat traffic and big wakes, and to my relief Jack took the helm. I felt very salty when we pulled up to the Lobster House dock and tourists gawked at our catch. Jack collected over $100 in cash for the fish, and handed Freddy and me each a $10 bill.

"We've got a little capital, now" he said. "I guess we'd better go ahead and catch our murderer. Time is of the essence if we're gonna find this character. We either need to get a fast little boat, or better yet, get airborne. I still got my pilot's license, but I don't think they'd rent me a plane at Woodbine, because my physical ain't up to date. And we can't use one of their pilots, for that would be letting the cat out of the bag, and we dare not spoil the thing by letting information slip. I guess I'll have to fire up the old Stearman and take my chances taking off out of my back field. It ain't been flown in seven year, but it's kept indoors, and I roll it out and start it ever now and then. You boys meet me at the dock at seven o'clock sharp tomorrow morning. It's too late today. I'll need help pushing it out of the barn, and I musn't let anyone know what we're up to."

That was the last thing anybody said till we got back to the dock. I felt pretty scarred, and figured Freddy did too.

"I hope he don't kill himself," Freddy said. "I guess we should help him, though. He threw in with us pretty heavy."

"How about if I stay over your house tonight, Fred? My folks will ask too many questions if we leave at seven o'clock, but we can just tell your dad we're going fishing at Clint's Mill. He's gone early anyway."

"Six-thirty, you mean. It takes a little time to get to the creek, and I have a feeling old Jack will be there early. His eyes lit up when he started talking about flying. Let's stop by your house and ask your mom."

CHAPTER EIGHT

The Old Stearman

Jack didn't drive his car like he drove his boat. He crept along about thirty miles an hour and built up a trail of about forty cars behind him by the time we got to Delmont, which was only about ten miles away. And that's not counting the cars that were able to pass him.

"I think we're developing a tail," he'd say as he hunched over the wheel and glanced accusingly at the rearview mirror. I was a nervous wreck by the time we got to his house and had a stiff neck from looking back across all the junk in the old car, sure any minute we were going to get rammed. It felt good to get off Route 47 and onto the back road, which had big fields on either side leading up to his place. It was a ramshackle house with a big barn out back and a lot of busted up trucks and tractors and homemade crane-like things, like my father's housemoving stuff only ten times junkier.

My heart sank when I saw all the junk, but when I saw the front of a big biplane through the open door of the barn, with its big radial engine, I got a scary thrill, like when you see a roller coaster and toy with the idea of going on it. The plane was yellow and kind of greasy, but it looked like it could fly. It was big. It had two open cockpits and said "restricted" in black letters under the back one. It had a "STP" sticker on the side, like a race car might have, and the propeller looked to be eight or nine

71

feet long. I was never real interested in airplanes, but I had to admit this was just about the coolest thing I had ever seen up close. I asked Jack why it sat with the front so high, higher than my head by a good bit, and Jack said that it was a tail dragger, which sounded pretty cool. Freddy had some books on planes, and said that this one looked like a World War I fighter plane. Jack said no, it was a 1942 P.T. 17 Boeing Stearman, with an R985 450 hp Pratt and Whitney engine, and he'd give the rest of the history lesson later. He had a fifty gallon drum of gasoline hanging from the rafters, which he had carried home on the tailgate of his car the night before, then chain hoisted up there so he could "gravity fill" the plane's gas tank, which was in the center of the top wing. He said it cost seventy dollars for the gas, but he didn't want to fly on short rations, because the plane had a powerful thirst. I felt bad when I heard he spent all that money and said Freddy and I would help pay for it.

"Well, I won't hold my breath, boy. And I don't want you stealin' no money. When I get my mind set to do something, little obstacles like money and danger ain't going to stop me. An' I ain't got no right to be scared anyway, since I'm living on borrowed time as it is. You're the one who should be scared, cause you're going up with me. We need at least four eyes. The other boy's gonna be ground crew. He'll stand on the edge of the field holding up the red flag, in case the wind changes when we get back."

Freddy acted disappointed, but I knew he was really relieved. We hadn't even considered one of us would be going up. I felt sick to my stomach, like when I went on the boat ride with Billy C. I felt bad enough already that I was sneaking around on my parents. I hoped I was doing the right thing, but this made it even worse. At least this guy was a friend, not like Billy C. But I had my doubts about how well he could fly after seeing how he drove. I didn't see any way out, though, after he'd spent seventy dollars on gas and all.

His wife came out of the house—a fat, ugly lady with no teeth and a big nose, not to mention a froggy voice. She said, "Are you gonna run that thing? Maybe I'll go to the store awhile, so I don't go deaf." I guess she thought he was just going to start it for us to show off or something. Anyway she didn't seem very concerned. For having a "Delmont Divorce," she and Jack seemed to get along alright. He asked her to help us push it out of the barn, and it took all four of us to do it. Then she left. One of the tires was soft and Jack blew it up, then he went all around the plane, wiggling parts of the wings and tail and little piano wires that seemed to be controls.

"Alright, climb in. We don't have time for a test run. I want to be airborne by the time anybody shows up. If anyone does, what's your name, tell them it's a young pilot taking old Jack for a ride."

I started to get in the back seat, but Jack said, "What— do you wanna fly it? Pilot sits in the back."

I felt kind of foolish. There were controls in the front, too, though: some pedals and levers and a thing like a gearshift in the middle. Jack handed me some goggles like

74

the ones my dad wears when he uses cutting torches, only they were clear, not green, and they fit pretty well. I turned around and saw he had a pair on, as well as a hat like Snoopy wears when he's after the Red Baron. He looked sort of comical, but I couldn't laugh. I thought I would wet my pants I was so scared. I did have to pee, too, but I wasn't feeling brave enough to say anything. I could just picture us crashing and burning in some field, and Freddy's dad hearing about it on the scanner.

"Strapped in, son?"

"Y-yeah."

"Ready?"

"I guess so."

"Clear prop."

"Prop clear," said Freddy, sounding official. He must have seen it in a movie.

R R R U N H . . . R R R U N H . . . R R R U N H, RRUNH-RAP-RAP—

It was the loudest motor I'd ever heard, worse than a truck without a muffler. The plane began to move, and we rolled all the way down to one end of the field, and Jack revved the engine while we sat still, till it was almost earsplitting. Then we started moving again and turned around to face the length of the field. I think we were facing northwest, towards Philadelphia, which was away from home and the creek. He raced the engine again, and we started really moving, bumping and bouncing along, and the plane kind of leveled out, till I could see where we were going.

Here was another situation I could hardly believe was happening, like when Tony got hit and I had to go call the cops. It had come about so fast—I had never dreamed I'd end up riding in the airplane. And I never could have imagined what it would be like. It was a massive, loud, dangerous machine. It gave me a whole new perspective on Jack. He had seemed dashing enough roaring along in his boat, but that hadn't been more than twenty miles per hour. And it certainly wasn't very scary. Just exciting. But this was too wild to be real. I couldn't understand him taking me up in it, unless he was real confident. I hoped he was, and just put all my faith into his ability to pull it off.

We went faster and faster, really bouncing, and it seemed like we were going to run into the trees at the other end. Then all of a sudden we lifted off the ground, which is where I left my stomach, and climbed up at a pretty steep angle. The engine was really roaring, but it wasn't as deafening up in the air. It was a terrific view—totally different than from how it looks on the ground. We banked around and flew over Jack's house, about three or four hundred feet high, I guess, and I waved to Freddy. I knew he was green with envy by now. I don't know how high we climbed to, but the trees looked like little bushes, and you could see as far as Wildwood.

I could see what must have been Route 47 off to my left, with little cars on it. The woods seemed huge. When we went over people's houses, which were mostly along the highway, their yards looked small and junky. Everything looked like some big hand had just set it there. The woods and marshes looked real graceful and nice. The houses and roads looked like when somebody hacks a piece out of a real nice looking cake. I figured if I lived through this trip, it was something I'd always remember, so I tried to keep track of everything I saw. I was glad Jack gave me the goggles, because the wind was really whipping my hair and shirt. Every once in a while I'd duck down into the cockpit for a little relief.

It seemed like no time before we were over the marshes of Dennis Creek. When we got to the creek we swooped down low and turned to the right, following its course towards the bay. It was scary when we swooped down, like a roller coaster, and it seemed like we were really going fast when we were down low. We were about forty or fifty feet high, maybe twice or three times as high as the little cedar trees on the islands. You could see everything perfectly clear, and as I say it looked a lot different from the air. I could see there weren't any secrets when you had a bird's eye view. It took about four or five minutes to go the whole length of the creek and out into the bay. You could see all the shoals and deep spots in the water. We criss-crossed over the marshes, following all the ditches, and I thought that if Ruth Fisher, the environmentalist, saw us she'd think we were spraying poison—after all it was a crop duster, and we were flying awful low.

We went up Sluice Creek, farther than the big boat could, past the bridge, and up a little ditch of the sluice. I thought I saw our boat. I turned around and pointed back towards it. Jack looped around, turning us just about sideways, and flew so low over where we'd just been that I though the wheels were going to touch. When we got to the highway, which didn't take too long at the speed we were going, Jack had to climb almost straight up to avoid the telephone wires. We looped around again in a bigger arc and came back at the boat crossways to the way we had been going. This time we could see it the whole time we approached it, and I could tell that the boat was just tied to a little stake in the ditch. The outboard and tank were on it, as well as what looked like an extra can of gas and the oars. But that was it.

I tried to yell back at Jack to tell him that the loot must be somewhere else, but he just kept squinting and pointed at his ear, shaking his head. He must have had the same idea, though, because he swooped along the edges of the woods and farther up the sluice looking. After a while he climbed back up high, maybe five hundred feet, and I figured he was heading for the barn. But then I realized he was angling back out towards the bay. When we got out to the mouth of the creek, he ducked down low and began skimming along the beach. He sure was different in the plane than driving his station wagon. He swept up and down the shore from the mouth of the creek to Reed's Beach, where the mouth of Bidwell's Ditch was, and back a couple of times. About the third time he tapped me on the shoulder and pointed down at the marsh behind the beach, which was fringed with bayberry bushes. There was a bright blue plastic tarp, with pieces of wood and rocks holding it down over what appeared to be a box and a few other things. And there was brush thrown over and around it, especially on the side toward the water. He tipped the plane up at a very scary angle as we went by so we could see better. From the air you could see it perfectly clear. Jack turned back over toward the marshes, and arched around till he was at a right angle toward the bay, directly over the tarp. When he got about a hundred feet out over the water, he dropped a Clorox bottle wrapped with clothesline (with a sash weight at the other end of the line, I found out later), to mark the spot. With that, we climbed back fairly high and headed back to Delmont. The whole trip only took fifteen or twenty minutes, but as Jack's house came into sight it seemed like we'd been gone a long time. We dropped right down over the tree tops and onto his field, touching down kind of hard, and bounced and jounced in a cloud of dust, till we stopped, almost at the other end, and turned around. Freddy came running out as we taxied back toward the barn. He'd been standing there with the "wind sock" as we came in, but he had been out of sight till we were just about landed, on account of being too close to the trees.

Jack spun it till it was facing tail-to the barn, and shut off the engine.

"She's a good old ship yet, boys. Never missed a tick. Controls was a little sloppy—some adjustin' would be in order. My eyes ain't perfect, but my reflexes ain't shot, either. Ain't up to doin' no crop dusting, I don't 'spect, but not bad for an old man."

"How'd you know to look along the beach when we didn't find the loot with the boat?" I asked, my head still buzzing.

"Just a guess, I guess. You see, every time I'm fishin' up in Dennis Creek cove, which is what that section is called, I think about how there's all that beach, and nobody ever goes to it. You have to cross about seven mile of marshes to get to it from the mainland. And people don't land boats on it, I guess because of the shoal water in front of it, except an occasional canoe over by Bidwell's Ditch. People don't go out in the bay in flat bottom skiffs much any more, but that's just what you want to get in over that shoal. And that's just what that Tobin boy has. Now tonight I suggest we ought to head out there on the tide in my boat and inspect that little spot.

The airplane ride filled my mind more at the time than the case at hand, but I tried to appear businesslike and interested in going out there in Jack's boat. At the same time, I thought maybe I'd done enough in one day.

"I think you're right, but I don't know about tonight. I don't want my folks getting suspicious, and Freddy's dad is pretty curious, too." In fact, I didn't know how much adventure I could stand. "During the day would be better for us, if you think we can wait till tomorrow."

"Not really, but I can't land the boat on that beach by myself. I don't think he's onto us, but he could move that stash any time. And he ain't completely stupid. If he heard us up there, or even heard about a plane flying around, he might get spooked. Well, if you think you're gonna get in trouble, we'll wait till tomorrow. I doubt the Tobin boy could get himself together any quicker than that if he wanted to. You remember where that boat is, don't you? Right up that little fork in the crick. I didn't mark that because

80

it might tip him off, and should be pretty easy to find. That beach is different, though. Just looks like a fisherman's float—there's dozens out there, though of course not exactly like mine. And the beach looks the same for five miles from the water, so natch'lly we had to mark it."

Jack dropped us off at the creek and headed back home. Freddy was about to bust to ask me about the flight in private. I laid it down pretty matter-of-factly, so Freddy wouldn't feel too bad. But my head was still whirling. A day before I hadn't cared a thing about planes. And now they seemed almost as important as boats, which was saying something. I'd always thought they were too dangerous, and besides, I'd never seen one up close or known anybody who had one. Freddy and I decided that once we got a good boat, the next thing we'd get was an airplane. Maybe Jack's, if he'd teach us how to fly it—what was he going to do with it, old as he was? Maybe he'd even take back payments. And when he retired from fishing, we might just want to buy his boat. Then we'd have everything just perfect.

Freddy said I was right not to go out tonight after Billy's stash. He thought we needed a breather. The more I thought about Billy taking the boat, though, the more I realized quick action was needed, and I was glad we had Jack in our corner. It would have been impossible to find that stuff without him. Freddy and I were in a pretty ticklish spot, especially me.

I went to sleep that night with the aerial views of the fields, the marshes, the woods, the lakes and the waterways I'd flown over that day criss-crossing in front of my eyes.

A couple of times I woke with a start when I dreamed the big old Stearman dropped out from under me, like in those dreams where you think you've stepped in a hole, usually just as you are falling asleep. Finally I drifted off at the wheel of Jack's big boat, rumbling smoothly down the creek. It was the first night in a while that I didn't have visions of Billy C. cutting off someone's head or knocking out Tony the crabber, or some such horrible thing as that.

CHAPTER NINE

The Skinny Dippers

The next morning Freddy woke me at seven o'clock. I threw on my shoes and we shot down to the creek on our bicycles. As we got closer we could see that something wasn't right. First we saw Jack's car, then we saw Jack. And Popeye, which was strange. But Jack's boat seemed to be gone. When we got over the bridge we realized that it wasn't exactly gone. I got a sick, spooky feeling when I saw it through the murky water resting on the bottom of the creek. The top of the cabin was only a couple of inches under the water, and an aerial was sticking out. You could see the windshield and cabin sides and the shiny bow rail down in the water, and barely make out the shape of the hull. It looked sad and kind of scary down there. Jack was in a real bad mood.

"Look's like your boyfriend Tobin's been here," Jack snapped at us as we pulled up on our bikes. I had the same feeling as soon as I saw it, but the first thing I was concerned about was that Jack would blame me for not going to get the stash the night before. I tried to make it seem like maybe it was providential.

"Maybe," I said, "but maybe it just happened. If that's the case, we're just as lucky we didn't go or we might be at the bottom of the bay right now." I didn't really believe this as I said it, and I hoped Popeye didn't twig to our secret, but when Jack agreed I felt a little better about it.

83

"I never even thought of that, boy. What-a-ya think, Popeye? Maybe it just happened."

"Fat chance, Pugh. I don't believe in coincidences. If you've seen the Tobin boy snoopin' around here, and I've seen him, then I say the Tobin boy did it. That boy ain't no good whatsoever. Him or that Dicky Meehan. I seen the two of them around here not too long ago. I don't know which one I like worse. Dicky ain't quite as dangerous, but he's more crazy. I feel sorry for his old man. Adopted two boys, then his wife died. The other one's alright. In the army. Only time that old Jed Meehan gets any rest is when Dicky's in jail or up the mental hospital. Maybe the best thing to do would be to just get Dicky and the Tobin boy together and put them out of their misery." Jack wasn't paying much attention to Popeye, and Freddy and I pretended not to be, but the part about Dicky Meehan scared me. He was crazy, but people said he was pretty smart, too. I thought what a horrible combination he and Billy C. would make.

"Well, I 'spect I know how to find out if it was an accident," Jack said. "I gotta borrow a big volume pump, and try to pump her out if the gun'nels come close enough to the surface at low tide. Just don't know whether I can keep her floatin' once I do get her up, dependin' on what sunk her."

Freddy and I decided it was just as well to leave him alone since his temper was going downhill again. We wouldn't have minded helping, except he was in such a bad mood, and told us to get lost. I couldn't help feeling guilty for not going out the night before, even though we

85

might have run across Billy C. and been in real trouble. Now Jack's boat was ruined, or at least needed lots and lots of work. Freddy said it wasn't us who sunk it so let's not get too upset. Freddy's not much for stewing on things that have already happened. If Billy did do it, though, he said, that means he's probably on to us, so let's lay a little low, which was a good idea. We rode our bikes home and hung around Freddy's because both his mom and dad were at work. We watched some game shows and part of a Tarzan movie, then Freddy said let's sneak back up to the creek by way of the railroad tracks. We had never seen Billy C. along the tracks. He always seemed to just walk up and down the roads. So the railroad tracks seemed relatively safe, and we would be walking by the pond on a hot day, which might provide an added bonus.

As we headed up the tracks we couldn't seem to keep our minds off Jack's boat and Billy C. In Freddy's house we were preoccupied with T.V. and all and so we felt pretty safe, but along the tracks we kept expecting Billy C. to jump out of the bushes any second. Once you get past the first couple of houses beyond Freddy's there aren't any more until you get past the creek and into Dennisville. It seems safe in the sense that you hardly ever see anybody, but naturally if you did see somebody you didn't want to you wouldn't have much luck calling for help. We were feeling kind of spooky, like we did when we saw our boat was gone and when we saw Jack's boat sitting on the bottom of the creek. When we got past the Route 83 overhead near the little pond, we heard some laughing female voices, and our spirits rose considerably.

We crept up quietly to the pond, but at first we couldn't see anything. It was real brushy so we figured there must be a path we didn't know about. We could hear what seemed to be two girls, and I judged that they were on the far side of the pond. We crawled back out of the brush and went along the tracks a ways to get a better vantage point. We saw some broken branches and followed them in to find a place where cherry trees hung over the bank, and there was a little sandy-muddy area with a lot of bare footprints. There were some clothes hanging over a couple of the lower branches. When we looked out through the branches we could see Gloria Hunt and Sandy Spinelli swimming over toward the other bank, which was only about seventy feet away. I would have believed Sandy Spinelli, but Gloria Hunt was in my class and was the biggest goody two-shoes, straight A's, safety-patrol type in the school. She had just her black underpants on, which we saw when she walked up on a sandbar with her back to us. We also noticed she had an excellent wedgie. She was short and had brownish-blond hair and looked very good with her clothes off. In fact, she looked better than she did with them on—and a lot different. I felt kind of like Buddy Langston, our local peeping tom, but I didn't want to leave before Sandy got up on the sandbar, too. Gloria went back down in the water, then Sandy, who is taller, and has real dark hair, did a kind of a dolphin flip that made her butt come up out of the water, and she wasn't wearing anything! Then I was sure I wanted to wait until they got up out of the water. Just then Freddy nudged me and handed me some clothes and a pair of sneakers. I saw he was also holding a pair of shoes and some clothes—

dungarees and a shirt. I was holding shorts and a shirt and underpants, so I figured I must have Sandy's stuff. Freddy motioned me to follow him. I didn't like it, but we went back in the bushes to a place a ways from where we'd just been and also had a good view of the pond. I whispered to Freddy that we were going to get into trouble this way, but he said no, it was just a panty raid, like they do in college all the time. Sandy's about sixteen, he said, so she might as well get used to it, and Gloria gets straight A's, so she ought to get used to it, too. Freddy was always so casual about stuff that it didn't seem like you could get in trouble from it. We sat there a while, and I began to think maybe he was right, maybe they'd just laugh and we'd give their clothes back, free show included. After all, they'd taken them off, not us. Before too long they swam back towards our side, laughing and talking. The bank was gently sloped so we got a nice show as they waded out toward the edge once they touched bottom. When they got pretty close to the shore they noticed their clothes were gone and they got real mean looks on their faces, especially Sandy, and started scanning the bushes. I could tell there wasn't going to be much laughing. Sandy scowled real nasty. Gloria looked nasty, but a little scared, too, and sat down in the shallow water, folding her arms over her breasts. Sandy just stood there knee deep, with her hands on her hips.

I guess we weren't too well hidden because she spotted us in a minute and shouted at us.

"Get out of there, you little perverts! You're gonna get it for this!"

It made me mad when she said "little" perverts. It made me kind of scared, too, because I knew things could get ugly, but I didn't want to just back down and look like a wimp. I could tell she wasn't going to back down too easy, either. Freddy skipped back up through the bushes onto the railroad bed and yelled, "Come and get us, ladies!"

It seemed like a good idea to get out in the open, so I joined him. Sandy came crashing through the bushes. I've never seen anything so spectacular. Gloria came shuffling along behind her, stepping gingerly and moving the briars with her hands. But not Sandy. She was all scratched up and really steaming. Freddy said, "Maybe you girls should invest in bathing suits." Sandy just looked at him real mean—she had just gotten up on the railroad bed—and then looked at me. I must have looked like I was in shock. She said, "You better enjoy it, because you're sure gonna pay for it, you little pervert."

I guess she saw that I was the one with her stuff, because she lunged at me and grabbed at the clothes. When she did, she kind of tripped on the edge of a railroad tie and scraped her foot and then her knee as she went down. I hadn't even realized I'd stepped back, but she wound up on her hands and knees right at my feet.

"Damn you!" she shrieked as she lunged at me again. I dropped her clothes, and she was kicking me and hitting me and clawing me all at once. She was very tough, and even though I felt bad doing it, I had to grab her head and twist it to get her off me. Meanwhile Gloria got into the spirit and came after me, but Freddy grabbed her from behind, and with very little trouble held her in a headlock.

89

I twisted Sandy around by the head so that her back was to me and I had her pinned down between the rails. It was the only way I could immobilize her. She was screaming and crying, and I had this terrible feeling in the pit of my stomach. Things had gone even worse than I'd feared. Here Freddy and I were holding two naked girls, one of which was hysterical and kind of bashed up, and we had their clothes. I knew nobody was going to want to hear the practical joke explanation.

"Please calm down, Sandy," I said. "I'm sorry. I'll let you up if you promise not to flip out again."

"Damn you, you slimy little idiot. You're in trouble now, you Joe Bass. Basshole. Kick him in the balls, Gloria, he's a nothing, that little Freddy. You guys are pathetic. Why didn't you just stay in the weeds and gawk."

She was hard to hold because she was soaking wet. I had a hold under her chin, so she talked with clenched teeth and had to spit the words out. Gloria looked scared and was crying, but Freddy still had a tight grip on her.

"Look, I'm sorry. I can't let you up if you're just going to attack me again. You can have your clothes. I'm sorry we did it." She was just breathing heavy now and not struggling and seemed to be calming down some as I talked. Then Freddy piped up.

"It's my fault, Sandy. Joe didn't want to do it. He said it was a bad idea. And don't call him Basshole. That's mean."

"And taking our clothes and fighting with us isn't?"

"Yeah, but you did the attacking, even if we goaded you a bit. Joe didn't attack you." For all Freddy's weak points and hair-brained ideas, like this one, he certainly was loyal.

"Look girls, we're sorry," I said. "It got a lot worse than we thought. You can call us all the names you want. We got it coming. Now how about we let you up and you don't attack us, and we'll forget the whole thing and not tell anybody."

"Not so quick," Gloria spoke up. "Why should you get off so easy? You give us twenty bucks, and we won't tell anybody. And you have to promise you won't tell anybody either."

"Wait a minute," Freddy said. "If you don't want anybody to know, why should we pay you not to tell."

"Medical expenses," Sandy said. "Anyway, I thought you were sorry. Now you're already trying to worm out of it." She was starting to relax, so I eased up my hold on her a little bit. She realized what I was doing and said "let me go," so I did, and she got up and brushed off the sand and rocks and started picking up her clothes. I went to help her, but she said "turn your back," so I did, and I saw Freddy had let go of Gloria, and she was putting on her clothes. Sandy did lean her hand on my shoulder to steady herself as she put her shoes on, which made me feel a little better. I saw I had a big scratch on my right arm and some little ones on my left hand, and my shins hurt and my nose hurt where she must have hit me or bumped me and I didn't even realize it. I could feel a scratch near my eye that burned when the sweat got on it. It's a funny thing about fights, you can sometimes feel the blows landing, but you don't really know how banged up you are till it's over and your pulse drops back down. I looked at Sandy and saw she had big scrapes on her elbows and a couple of cinders and stones buried in her skin. It looked very nasty. She was trying to put on a sneaker, and I saw her toes where she caught them on the railroad tie had skin hanging off and were bloody. I felt sick to my stomach.

"Sorry about your foot and stuff. Do you thing you should go to the doctor?" I was leaning down looking at the foot when I said this, and she leaned up and smacked me right in the face.

"You're not sorry, you little creep. You feel bad now, but you'll get over that quick enough. You got to see me and Gloria naked and wrestled with us and humiliated us, and you know nothing's going to happen to you because Gloria would get in trouble if her parents found out she was skinny dipping. And you'll probably tell all your little friends how big my boobs are. But I might tell anyway and leave Gloria out of it. I'll have to explain these cuts somehow, and I bet they'd believe me over you if I said Gloria wasn't here. Or we could say you forced us. You'd be in trouble then, huh? What-a-ya think now, Basshole? Was it worth the thrill?"

"Look, I'll pay you for the doctor, if you want. I've got some money on me. Five dollars. I'll get you some more. I could get maybe a hundred. The doctor bill couldn't be much more than that."

"I got two dollars on me," Freddy said and handed them to Sandy. Sandy took my five dollars and handed Gloria the two dollars from Freddy—fair distribution based on who did the most work, I guess.

"I'll think about what I'm gonna do. It's gonna be something. Gloria and I got to talk it over."

As they walked off towards home Freddy and I couldn't seem to look at each other. We both knew how stupid it had been to take their clothes.

"It's my fault," Freddy said. "They never would've got so mad if we just watched."

"Yeah, but I could've said no."

"You did."

"But I didn't stick to it. I couldn't help going along. I just wanted to see them come after us. Have them at our mercy, I guess, because of the way they're too good for us at school. We went too far, though; they had a right to flip out. I guess I'm not much better than Billy C.

"Well, you didn't want to hurt them, like Billy would. Sandy went nuts. There's no way we could have expected that. I guess it was awful mean, though."

"She didn't take no crap, though," I said. "I don't ever want to tangle with her again. She went at it whole hog, all or nothing. She was a little mad, though. Didn't think about what she was doing. That's why I was able to tie her up."

As if we didn't have enough trouble already, now I had this escapade to worry about. At the same time I was still worrying about Jack's boat and Billy C. What if Billy C. did sink it? That meant we had dragged Jack into it, and it was mainly our fault that Jack's way of making a living was gone. And our boat was gone, too, which in a way was the least of our troubles. I tried to just worry about Jack's boat and Butterfly, but I couldn't get that poor scraped-up Sandy out of my mind. I had the feeling of dread, that pit in my stomach, where I kept thinking if only we'd used our heads and left their clothes alone, none of that ugly stuff would have happened. We bagged the idea of going to the creek. We went back and split up by Freddy's house, and I went on home. I had forgot about the scratches, and when my sister Kate saw me, she said, "Oh my God, what happened to you? Were you in a fight?"

"N-no," I said. "I rode my bike into a hedge."

"When?"

"Just a while ago."

"Well your bike's been here all afternoon."

Whoops, I thought. Better think fast. Time's a-wastin'.

"Yeah, well, I was on Freddy's bike."

"You didn't remember what bike you were on? You were in a fight, weren't you? That's alright. I won't tell Mom. Did you win?"

"Yeah, I guess. Thanks, Kate. Let's drop it for now, O.K.? I'll tell you about it pretty soon, though, soon as I can."

Kate was good about keeping secrets. She was worried about the bigger boys beating me up when I got to high school, because she thinks they pick on Dennis Township kids when they get shipped over to Middle Township. As long as she didn't know I was fighting with a girl, I knew she'd stick up for me.

Once again, as seemed to be happening so often lately, my head was swimming from one awful subject to another. I pictured Billy C. catching me or Freddy somewhere and cutting our heads off. And I thought about Jack standing on the bank, looking at his sunken boat, with his hands on his hips and his little hunched back and skinny neck and his sad little eyes. He makes his living with that boat, I thought, and I dragged him into this Butterfly caper, which was really none of my business in the first place, and nine chances out of ten Billy C. was onto us and sunk the boat. Then I pictured poor Sandy Spinelli with the skin hanging off her toes, wet and naked, with big red splotches on her from fighting and the stones embedded in her knees and elbows, and me pinning her down and prying her head back. I felt like I had to do something, but I didn't know what. I wanted to call Jack on the phone and tell him I'd help fix his boat, but somebody might hear me, and anyhow he'd probably just tell me to go back to my tinker toys.

So I called Leon to see if he had any ideas about Sandy and Gloria. Nobody's listen in if they heard me calling him, and he was always real loyal and glad to help if he could, and pretty smart, too.

"I don't know, Joe," he said. "This is a pretty bad one. At least they're not hurt too bad. And Sandy's older'n you. Gloria might be too embarrassed to raise a stink, and probably'll do whatever Sandy says. The best thing to do is lay low for a while. If they don't raise a fuss right away, they're probably not going to—that's my guess.

"Another choice might be to go and talk to one of them. Sandy'd be the best, of course. If she's calmed down some you might be able to straighten it out before anything happens just by apologizing."

We talked some more and I felt pretty good afterwards. It was kind of like talking to a grownup, but not having to worry about getting yelled at.

CHAPTER TEN

Sandy

After supper I slipped out and walked down to Sandy's house, which was almost a mile down the road. I figured any minute Billy C. would jump out of the shadows and strangle me from behind. I could actually feel his fingers around my neck squeezing. I sneaked along in the dark, jumping at every sound. When I got to Sandy's house I didn't know what to do. If I went and knocked on the door her father might answer it and kill me if he knew what happened. And even if he didn't, Sandy would probably slam the door in my face. I had brought twenty dollars in an envelope, which I intended to put in the mailbox, but I decided nobody would know what it was for unless I put Sandy's name on it, and if I did that, she might get in trouble.

I walked back and forth for a little while, but after my adventures earlier in the day the last thing I needed was to get caught snooping around somebody's house, so I turned and headed back home. It was about 8:30 when I got home and my mom asked where I was because Freddy had called. I said out on a walk, which mom didn't look too sure about, and she said she had asked Freddy how his bike was since I'd crashed it into the bushes, and he'd said, oh, fine, but he didn't seem to know where the "crash" had taken place. I was happy that Freddy was even quick-witted enough not to say, "What crash? Joe never crashed my bike." He wasn't naturally sneaky, like me, but I could see I was rubbing off on him a little.

I went in and called him, but there wasn't much we could say with all those ears around me. Then about nine o'clock Kate signaled me into the kitchen and said Sandy Spinelli was outside and wanted to talk to me. She said it was private so she didn't want to come in. She wasn't real good friends with Kate since Kate was two years older, but they knew each other and got along O.K. Kate raised her eyebrows up and down and said she wanted to hear about this later as I slipped out the back door.

As soon as I was out the door, Sandy popped out of the shadows and was holding out a five dollar bill.

"I walked up and down, but I didn't have the nerve to knock. Then I saw Kate in the kitchen window and went up and tapped on the glass. I hope I didn't scare her. She must think I have the hots for you. That's a laugh. Look, you were a real creep to me today, but I don't think you meant for it to go so far. I never should have taken your money. And I shouldn't have said I'd say that you two forced us. I'll get that two dollars off Gloria for your little jerk friend."

"You know what? I just got back from walking up an down in front of your house. I wanted to apologize, but I was afraid you might tell your dad on me if I came around bothering you. I was a real creep today. I'm sorry. I really am. If somebody did that to my sister, I'd want to kill him. It was s'posed to be a joke, but in my heart I knew it was too mean when we first took the clothes.

I'm sorry we saw you two naked. I mean, for your sake. You know, ah, you look great, ah, I'm sorry you got hurt. I'll do anything you want to make it up to you."

"Take off your clothes, and let me slam you to the ground, and make you cry, and then I'll let Gloria come look at you and we'll all have a big laugh."

"Well, almost anything. I am sorry I did it. I'm in trouble already with something else, which I can't tell you about, though it's not something I did wrong. But that's not your problem. Is Gloria still pretty mad?"

"Oh, man. Poor Miss Goody Two-Shoes. I really teased and bugged her before she'd take her clothes off. We've been down there three times, and this is the first time she went in naked. Well, she had her underpants on. I took mine off the second time. It really feels good, as long as no punks come along and take your clothes. Now she's so mad at me. She says she can't go out of her house knowing you two boys saw her like that. I told her somebody's gonna have to see you naked sooner or later, but she said she was waiting for her breasts to grow before that happened, and she hoped it would be with 'that special someone,' not two local nerds. She's such a yummy. She'll get over it, though. She didn't make a fool out of herself quite like I did."

"You didn't make a fool outta yourself. You put us guys to shame. You didn't take any crap."

"I am sorry you guys did that to us, but I was partly to blame. I guess we were asking for trouble, peeping-tom wise, I mean. But you didn't have to take our clothes. You could have been happy with your little thrill of seeing us."

"This prob'ly sounds like crap coming from me," I said, "but that was awful dangerous. If Billy C. Tobin or some ex-convict walking the tracks had seen you, you could have been in real trouble."

"So, what, you taught me a lesson?"

"I didn't mean that. But when you see how mean some people can be, and I have, you see that what I did was like nothing. Not that it lets me off the hook or anything. If you knew what I knew, you'd see what I mean."

I hadn't even noticed we were walking, but we were almost down to her house. She told me to sit down on a fence we were near and tell her what I meant. I got a sudden jolt, realizing I'd let too much slip, so I figured I'd just have to clam up.

"C'mon, Joe. Now you got me curious. What happened? I'm on the edge of my fence rail."

"I'd rather not say. It might jeopardize an investigation I'm involved with."

"*You're* involved with? What are you, a junior detective? Did somebody's bike get stolen?"

"Don't be like that," I said. "It's serious. You're a very nice girl, Sandy, and I'd rather not get you involved in this."

"Remember you said you'd do anything I wanted to make it up to me? Well, this is it. Spill it."

"Aw, c'mon. I know I said it. But I just can't. I'm sworn to secrecy."

"Swear me to secrecy. I'll cross my heart."

"Sorry." I felt real bad, going back on my word, which my father says never do under any circumstances. He also says to hang tough, stick to your guns. He has a lot of sayings. I was caught in the middle. And that "cross my heart" line made me think of how Sandy was dressed the last time I'd seen her. Here was a pretty, popular sixteen year old girl, talking to me. My heart told me to do whatever I had to, just to keep her attention. My head told me to hang tough.

"You said anything," Sandy said. "Tell you what. I'll give you a choice. If you take off all your clothes, including your shoes and socks, and give them to me, and trust me with them, I'll let you off the hook. I promise I'll give them back and we'll be even."

The way she put it, it sounded fair, but I just couldn't bring myself to do it. I smelled a trap.

"I don't know," I said. "I'm in a mess now, and I've caused plenty of trouble. This looks like a way to cause more."

"C'mon, chicken. Or else tell me your secret. I can't be any fairer than that. I promise not to laugh."

As if I wouldn't feel goofy enough with my clothes off in front of her. Now she was making fun of me.

"Don't get mad, Joe. I didn't mean to put you down."

Another female that could read minds. Or at least faces.

I'm sorry about calling you Basshole. I know you must hate it. It's just that you saw me naked today, and it isn't fair. There's no way I can take it back. I thought maybe you'd be willing to even the score."

"I'd like to, but isn't there an easier way?"

"An easier way? At first you said you'd do anything, but now you've turned down the first two things that came up. I was wrong to take your money, and I'm sorry I did it, and that's why I came to see you. But I wasn't as wrong as you were, taking our clothes and teasing us with them. You made a joke out of us, and tried to make us ashamed of ourselves. It was partly our fault, but it was mostly yours. I know you feel bad. But do you feel bad enough to do something about it, or are you just sorry for yourself 'cause you're in a bad spot?"

"Let me think," I said. She was right again. It sure is a lot easier to say "I'll do anything" than it is to back it up.

"All right," I said. "I'll take off my clothes." I could feel my heart pounding and my face getting red. I felt about two feet tall. It was probably dark enough so she couldn't see my face getting red, but it was only a couple of days off a full moon, so that's about all she was going to miss. I took off my shoes and handed them to her. I felt kind of flushed. Then after a little pause, I took off my shirt.

"You feeling a little stupid, Joe?"

"A little," I said.

I unzipped my pants and started pulling them down.

"Hold on. Now would you rather tell me your secret?"

"I'd rather. But I can't. I'm afraid it might do you harm just to know it." I left my pants where they were.

"So you're gonna take your clothes off and leave yourself at my mercy? It must be some secret. Here." She handed me my shirt and shoes. "Put these on before the mosquitoes eat you. You've proved your point. You didn't chicken out. I guess you really are sorry. Today when we were fighting you let me loose as soon as I gave you the chance. I guess I should return the favor. Now you still owe me. No, I'm just kidding. It would be a sneaky sort of way to satisfy my curiosity. Ulterior motives, isn't that what they call it? You sure didn't look like you were enjoying yourself. It's nice that you thought enough of me to be willing to go through with it. Did you think I was sleazy to ask you to do it?"

"Not really. It was fair enough. I'm the one who must seem like a pervert. I really did feel bad doing what I did to you. Even for spying on you."

"Oh, I was that bad, huh?"

"No, no. I don't mean that at all. You were, I mean you are beautiful."

"With or without clothes?"

"Both, well, you know. You're classy, too. I won't tell anybody what I saw. But I won't forget it, either."

"Well, that's sweet, I think."

We suddenly seemed very close. Then she said, "Now tell me about your secret."

I had no will to say no to her. What could I do, tell her I didn't trust her? She was so easy to talk to, when she wanted to be, and I had never dreamed I'd ever even have a conversation with her. I felt a little bit like I did when dad let me have two beers on New Year's Eve. It was like I couldn't quite control what I was saying. Well, I could, partially, but stuff was coming out faster than I could keep track of it.

"Promise, cross your heart and hope to die," I said. "I'm trusting you. You can't tell a soul."

She looked quite serious and lovely. I told her about our boat, about the fire and Butterfly, about my ride with Billy C. and what he said about killing the guy and raping the girl, about his stash, about him knocking out Tony, about Jack and the plane ride, Jack's boat getting sunk, and a few other things. She asked if she could help us, and I said it was really too dangerous, but if I could think of anything she could do that wouldn't put her at any risk, I'd tell her. She said she believed Billy C. killed Butterfly and raped the girl, because she had heard that Billy C. had raped his retarded cousin, and he had even made rude suggestions to Sandy herself. I told her to be careful when she goes out, and definitely no more skinny-dipping at the pond, and I told her to tell Gloria I was sorry and so was Freddy.

"You're a pretty good little guy, Joe. If somebody was gonna see me naked, I guess I'm just as glad it was you as anybody. I don't mean *little* guy. Keep me up to date on your investigation. And be careful. Call me if you want, and tell me what's happening."

"How do your arms and knees and foot feel?" I asked.

"They sting and hurt if I stretch the skin any. But I'll live. I told my mom I went over the handlebars on Gloria's bike."

"Haa—I told my mom I crashed Freddy's bike into a bush."

She leaned over and kissed me real quick on the forehead and said "see ya" and trotted off toward her house. A little gingerly, I'd say, probably because of her skinned knees. I was in a daze for a while from that little kiss—it imprinted itself on my forehead and kind of shocked my brain—as I walked back home. The back of my brain was nagging at me for spilling my guts to her, but the front part was buzzing with approval. It was the good angel and the bad angel they talk about at Sunday School—each one trying to influence you, but in this case I couldn't tell which was the good one and which was the bad one. I decided to keep our little confab a secret from Freddy and Jack for the time being, just to avoid any complications. My sister Kate was another story.

It was after ten-thirty when I got home, and my mom and dad were already in bed.

"I covered for you," Kate said. "I told Mom you were running an errand for me. Now let's talk."

"I can't Kate. Not right now, anyway. But I will later —as soon as I can. Thanks for covering me."

"Now be careful Joe. Don't make too much of things. I don't want to see you get your heart broken at such a tender age, sonny boy."

"I won't," I said, and headed up for my room. But I sure felt funny—not bad, really, maybe a little indigestion, like when you're waiting to take a final exam, with the butterflies in your stomach and all. I kept picturing Sandy—her hair, her nose, her eyes, her chest...

"Snap out of it," I told myself. "You have a murder case to solve." I finally drifted off to sleep, but I took the pictures of Sandy with me.

CHAPTER ELEVEN

We Rescue Jack's Boat

The next morning I found out that my dad had heard about Jack's boat sinking.

"I stopped by the creek when I heard about it, 'cause I was afraid the old bird was gonna try and pin it on you," my dad said. "He surprised me, though. Just about the first thing he said was, 'Don't worry, Bass. I know it wasn't your boy. Him and young Chance are good boys, that I'm sure of.'" Then he said something about being in a fix for making a living with no way to get to his pots and nets. That was it. No real cussing or anything. He looked so sad. Just stood there with his hands on his hips lookin' down at his sunken boat, shakin' his head once in a while and talking to himself. I s'prised myself by saying I'd come down today, bein's it's a Saturday, and maybe bring my power truck and a pump and take a crack at raising the old tub. You and Freddy interested in such doin's?"

Indeed I was, and I knew Freddy would be. I had never even dreamed of a solution as good as this one. By now, Freddy and I were both too scared to go down to the creek by ourselves, but who could be scared riding with my dad in his big truck? I had wanted to help Jack, of course, but I'd felt like I'd be useless. I never even considered that my dad might get involved, especially considering the way he had run down Jack to me. But now, suddenly, things were falling into place. And I knew

Jack wouldn't spill the beans. I called Freddy, and he was over in about the same time it took me to find my shoes.

Dad's power truck is the biggest truck he has. It's a '53 Mack tractor, which was made extra heavy duty for hauling big cranes and equipment. It has a fifth wheel for pulling trailers, and it also has a big cable-winch behind the cab, which is why it's called a power truck. He uses the winch to slide houses, and when he wants to lift his big I-beams he puts on the "tripod," which is three big pipes that hook onto the back of the truck and come to a point at the top. He can adjust it till it's almost straight up about fifteen feet high, or lay it way out back behind the truck.

Dad already had the tripod hooked up, and he loaded on a six-inch steel beam about twelve feet long, and two big nylon straps. Then he threw on the gasoline power pump he uses to clear out water from underneath the house he's going to move.

As big as the truck is, it has a very narrow cab, and Freddy and I had to jam together in the passenger seat. The Mack has two gearshifts and twenty forward speeds, and a real mellow sounding engine. I felt as safe as if I were in an army tank roaring down to the creek. When we got there Jack was standing on the cabin of the boat, which was sticking up a little bit out of the water. It was about half tide and coming in. Popeye was standing on the edge of the bulkhead, looking stinky.

"Hey, Pugh, you old prune," my dad said as he climbed down out of the cab. "Can't catch no fish that way." He pulled the straps from the truck. "See if you can work

109

them under the front and back. The boys'll help you. Maybe the mud'll let them slide in a ways." Freddy and I and Jack jumped right down into the back of the boat, which was under water a ways. The water was cold and Freddy and I were jumping around and laughing, but not Jack. He went right to work. The sides of the boat were about two feet under, so we were in over our waists. Jack ducked under and poked the center of the strap under the rudder and keel with a stick, while Freddy and I sawed back and forth with the ends to work it on in. When it was in place, we tied ropes to the ends and handed them up to my dad. We did the same thing up front. My dad backed the truck up to the bank, and by now the I-beam was hanging from the tripod. There was a shackle at each end—it was hanging straight across—and we lined it up lengthwise to the boat and hooked the straps to the ends. We climbed up on the bank and my dad clunked the winch into gear, then the cable tightened and she started to raise.

"Bring 'er right on out!" Freddy said, very excited.

"Oh no, son," my dad said. "Mr. Pugh would shoot me for that, 'cause she'd come to pieces." He stopped it just as the gun'nels cleared the surface of the water. Then he and Jack wrestled the pump off the truck and stuck the suction line in the boat. When it got primed, it shot a great, huge geyser of water straight up and nearly drowned us, so they had to hook a firehose to the outlet and tie it to a piling so it wouldn't whip around. Each time the water level went down a little bit my dad lifted the boat the same distance, till in about an hour it was riding up nice and high like it was supposed to. The deck hatches had floated away, as well as the engine box. Otherwise the boat looked O.K., although awful muddy, and a lot of reeds and stuff were stuck all over. Jack said the motor might be O.K. if he tore her down fast enough, but it would need lots of work. He looked around under the deck and saw that the seacock had been screwed out.

"She was sunk deliberate," Jack said. "Someone pulled the plug." It was just about the first thing he'd said since we got there, outside of "right there", or "that's it", as he and dad and we boys worked together. Once Jack got the plug back in, Freddy and I got the last bit of water out of the hull with the hand pump that was mounted up towards the front of the boat, while Jack used his soggy tools that had been sunk with the boat to unbolt the engine. It seemed like no more than twenty minutes before he and my dad had it ready to lift out. They hooked a chain from the boom on the truck to the motor and cranked the motor up and swung it onto the back of the truck.

"Run 'er up to your barn, Jack? I expect you'll want to get her tore apart right quick," my dad said.

"If it ain't too much trouble, Bass. I owe you a lot already. Woulda took me three year to do that by myself. I doubt my power truck would make it down here, even if it would run. Don't 'spect it's been run in ten year. Don't 'spect it has a motor in it no more, come to think of it. Sold that to Ed Hillary for his irrigation pump. Yeah, looks like I'm in your debt pretty heavy."

"Don't mention it, old Jack. I needed a chance to try out the nylon straps. That don't mean a bushel of crabs would go unappreciated around Labor Day if you're back in business by then."

"You got it boy, even if me and Popeye's got to swim out and hand pick 'em."

I had forgotten about Popeye, but he'd been standing around there the whole time, never saying a word. He smiled a little when Jack said about swimming after the crabs, but it didn't help his looks any. Even out here in the fresh air you could smell him if you got close, which I didn't do any more than I had to.

My dad had a good time snooping around Jack's old relics of machinery when we got up to his place. There's nothing my dad likes better than a good junkyard, the older the better, and Jack's place came pretty near qualifying.

"Don't s'pose the old Stearman goes up to often nowadays," my dad said as he looked over Jack's airplane. If only he knew, I thought. Jack certainly wasn't giving out any hints. "I used to love to watch you swoop around them fields when I was a boy, Jack. I prob'ly sniffed about forty gallons of DDT watching you."

"You wasn't one of them boys that sat in the edge of the woods and heaved rocks at the plane when it climbed up by the trees, was you, Bass?"

"No, not me. I was an admirer. I always wanted to learn to fly one of these things."

"Ain't too late, Bass. Plenty of fellers your age learn to fly. If you want to learn in a man's plane, I can make you a hell of a deal on this old ship."

"It's too late for me, Jack. And too expensive. I can't even afford a boat, let alone a plane. And my wife'd cut my head off if I came home and told her I'd just bought an old crop duster."

"Much money as a house mover makes? Let me tell you, there ain't nothing quite like flying. Ah, well, I guess you're right. Who needs another expensive, dangerous hobby? Being married's bad enough."

"Amen, old Jack."

For being in such a hurry to tear down his engine, Jack sure didn't mind chewing the fat with my dad. He was as interested in house moving as my dad was in fishing and logging and airplanes. They discussed old winch trucks they'd known and loved, and boats and planes. My dad told Jack about some of his house moving adventures.

"...Yeah, Jack. Got that house on the road—the middle of Landis Avenue, and the guy havin' it moved came tearing up and said, 'I don't have the lot. The deal fell through!' I could have killed the little fool. Now what was I gonna do? I left the house in the middle of the road, and the boys and I had lunch a while, trying to think of a place to put it. We didn't want to get too far down the road with it, in case the guy never came up with a lot, but good Lord, we couldn't leave it in the middle of Landis Avenue forever. So we turned her up a side street and headed for the ballfield—the only hard ground in Sea Isle that ain't got a house or cars parked on it. The next day, we seen there was a parking ticket on the windshield. For the offense, the 'other' box was checked off—'explanation: parking house on ballfield.'"

"That's a pretty good one, Joe. I ever tell you about the time me and Ed Winston got the job of dropping leaflets from an airplane? Well sir, that was back in my heavy drinkin' days, and me and Ed had a snootful over at Lew Holt's. We wasn't in no condition to sit on a barstool, let alone fly an airplane. But we figured between the two of us, we could maybe handle it. We staggered down the airport and climbed into Ed's J3 Cub and took off. They was in about fifteen packets that weighed about three pounds a piece, all taped together, and we just flopped them in with us. We was s'posed to flutter them out like ticker tape over the beaches—advertising the Wildwood Boardwalk, I think—nowadays you couldn't get away with it. They'd call it pollution. Anyway, on the way over to the shore Ed buzzed Francis Meerwald's chicken houses— killed about a hundred hens, I think, and Francis was some put out. If that wasn't bad enough, when we got over the beach, Ed just heaved the packets out whole, down on the beach, one at a time. People must of thought they were getting bombed. Never heard about anybody getting hurt by them, but it wasn't 'cause Ed didn't try. Then as we flew back over town Ed threw out his beer bottles. You'd lose your license for that nowadays, I expect. As it was, I never heard of Ed getting any more work with them leaflets."

They told stories for more than an hour. I'd heard a lot of my dad's before, but it was still fun listening to him, and it made me feel proud when Jack would act impressed, which he wasn't putting on—Jack wasn't that way.

My spirits were a whole lot more springy after this episode. I was real proud of my father—he could get so much done and make it seem so easy—then act like it was nothing. But old Jack knew it wasn't just nothing. That's what made me feel so good.

But after sitting around a while at my house with Freddy, I got to thinking about what a scary situation we boys were still in. I wanted to ask Jack what we should do next, but I didn't want to disturb him from getting back on his feet with his boat and all. I knew he couldn't leave his nets and crab pots out too long, or they'd get wrecked in the weather. Freddy and I stewed about it, and cooked up all kinds of outlandish plans, like you do when you look at a tricky situation from the comfort of home and let your imagination get cranking. We thought of things like "borrowing" the Mosquito Commission's helicopter, or enlisting the help of the Hell's Angels, but once in a while the reality of the thing would hit us, and our little bit of relief would go all to pieces. After all, we were just two young kids who could actually do very little about a dangerous guy like Billy C. without an adult to help us. That is, unless we wanted to get into even worse trouble. I was starting to think I better spill my guts to my dad, but I still couldn't bring myself to do it because of all the ruckus it would cause, and I wasn't too sure it would solve anything. I knew it would be sure to get Freddy and me into a whole lot of trouble, though, not only with our parents, but maybe Billy C. too.

The phone rang and I went over to answer it. My mom said, "They'll probably just hang up. I got three calls like that already."

CHAPTER TWELVE

Adventure At Sea

"Hello?" I said.

"That you, Joe?"

"Yeah."

"It's me, Sandy. I hung up on your mom a couple of times. I hope she isn't too mad. I had to talk to you, but I didn't know what to say to her. I was embarrassed. I thought maybe she'd get the wrong idea or something."

"uh-huh." I didn't know what to say without giving away who I was talking to. I'd never hear the end of it if I did.

"Listen. I've got an idea," she said. "And I think you're in a lot of danger. Meet me down by the railroad tracks by Freddy's."

"O.K. See you in a bit."

"Who was that, Joe?" my mother asked. I was sure she could tell it wasn't Freddy just by the tone of my voice.

"Goofy Leon Berman," I said. "Wants me to come see his new chemistry set." It seemed to me that if I acted like I didn't want to go it was easier to act natural about it."

"Leon Berman? Since when is he calling you about his chemistry set?" Uh-oh, I thought. She smells a rat.

"Well, I must say it's a nice change to see you expanding your interests a bit." Whew, off the hook. "It won't hurt you to be a little nicer to Leon. Maybe his enthusiasm for school work will rub off on you just a little."

Poor Leon. I did neglect him. Now I would have to go see him. My mom will want to know how his old Aunt Thelma is doing, I thought, but that was O.K. I told myself I'd go see him later today or tomorrow.

When I saw Sandy, my stomach kind of jumped. She looked very lovely and was kind of keyed up, which didn't hurt her appearance any. She had real pleasant, sparkly eyes, especially when she smiled or was excited.

"Hi, Joe. I thought about Old Man Pugh's boat getting sunk. I bet it was Billy C. I think he probably knows you and the old guy are after him. I was up all night thinking about different things he might do to you—and I kept having these gruesome visions of—well, never mind."

"Thanks."

"But listen. I think we better do something. And it can't be calling the cops. If we do that and they don't lock him up real tight, then you're really in for it."

"Wait a minute, Sandy. 'We' better do something? I don't want you involved in this. It's just too dangerous. You saw what happened to Jack for getting involved already. I'm sorry I told you 'cause now I got you worried. I wish you could just try and forget about it."

"Oh, I'm a little waif, and you're a big, strong man. I think I can stick up for myself."

118

"I know you can. I wasn't cutting on you. I just don't want to see you get hurt. If something happened to you, I'd never forgive myself for getting you involved. You're much too pretty to get tangled up in this nasty stuff."

"Did I see you blushing, Joe?"

"Did I see you, Sandy?"

"C'mon now. Don't start getting a crush on me. I'm too mature and sophisticated."

"I'm not getting a crush. Is it all right if I like you and don't want to see you get hurt?"

"I'm O.K. I'm sorry. But I've come up with a plan. Just listen to me and if you don't like it I won't bother you any more."

"Alright. But you're allowed to bother me whether I like the idea or not."

"Listen. You know where Billy C.'s stash is, and you can only get to it in a boat, right? Any Billy C.'s got your boat. And as far as we know, that's his only way to get there, too. All we have to do is take back your boat, get the stash, and we should be able to get enough evidence to nail him. And he won't be able to come after us 'cause we'll have the boat."

"'Us?'" 'We'll have the boat?'"

"Just let me finish. My father saw Billy C.'s father at Tommy Holmes' and Billy C.'s father said Billy C. had to go to court tomorrow about crashing up his old man's truck, and his old man said, 'Billy C.'ll be there if I have to take him in pieces. I ain't getting my insurance took away because of that little loser."

"Now, all we got to do is take advantage of the situation. We'll get the stash and put Billy C. out of transportation at the same time.'"

"That does sound fairly good, though fairly risky. Anyhow, you can't come."

"You think you and little Freddy will be better off without me?"

"Prob'ly not. But it will be one less person to get killed if Billy happens to miss his court date. I agree we've gotta do something, but I'm not letting you get caught in this ridiculous mess."

"Well, I think maybe you boys could use my protection." She was carrying a pocketbook, which had struck me kind of strange for a meeting like this, and now she zipped it open and pulled out a huge revolver, a .44 special like Dirty Harry uses. "It's my dad's," she said. "He keeps it locked up in a safe in the basement, but I know where the key is."

"Holy cow, Sandy," was all I could say.

"What, would you rather Billy C. had the upper hand? I know how to shoot. I've been out to the gravel pit a couple of times with my dad for target practice. It's loaded, don't worry."

"That's not what I was worried about." This was almost as scary as Billy C., to see Sandy waving this loaded cannon around.

"What are you gonna do, carry your pocketbook on this mission?" I asked.

"No. I'll ditch that. I'll just stick the gun in my pants in the back. They're pretty tight. Then I'll wear a loose shirt. I just brought the pocketbook to show you."

This was getting scary. Freddy and I had imagined being armed in our pipe dream attacks on Billy C., but really having this gun, and sneaking it, that had me shook. It made the whole thing a lot scarier, and I felt like I'd slipped another foot down a well shaft.

"Well, I guess you really want to do it, and I can't talk you out of it. I hate to think about you getting involved in this, but I'm out of arguments. I guess I'd seem like a chicken if I came up with any more excuses."

I went and rounded up Freddy, and outlined the plan. Freddy said to make sure Sandy doesn't boss us around too much, but otherwise had no objections to her coming along. He seemed a little surprised that she knew so much, but was a good enough sport to keep it to himself.

The three of us met at the railroad tracks by Freddy's the next morning, and we followed the tracks on down south for about two miles until we were almost at the head of Sluice Creek. We cut west through the heavy cat briars and underbrush in the woods along the edge of the swamp. It was so thick, we finally went right out onto the marsh and promptly sunk in the mud halfway to our knees. Sandy lost a shoe and we couldn't find it in the muck, but she didn't complain. The mud was black and stinky, and the going was slow. I was sure Billy C. had a more direct route, but we couldn't find it. Some parts of a marsh are as solid to walk on as your front lawn, and have those red saltworts growing on them, but of course we had to go through the real soft mush, with high marsh grass and plenty of streams running through it. The location of the boat seemed obvious and easy to get to when I saw it from the air, but every piece of ground we covered looked like all the others from down here, and I kept expecting to see it over every hump of grass. My crew was getting grumpy and beginning to doubt my navigating ability when we finally came upon a sluice big enough to float a boat on. We followed it back towards the woods and were almost on top of the boat when we found it.

The motor started on the second pull, and there was plenty of gas, so we piled in, with me at the controls, and started putt-putting out of the sluice. There was only about four inches of water in the boat so we knew Billy C. had been there to bail it out in the last day or so. By the time we were out in Sluice Creek Freddy and Sandy had the boat bailed down to less than an inch of water, and we started making good headway. With all the weight it was leaking a lot, though. You could see the water coming in along the chines, so they had to stay on top of the bailing.

It was hot out so we dangled our feet in the water off and on to wash the mud off and cool down. We also rinsed our shoes off, which had got pretty well mud-caked, and set them up on the bow deck to dry in the sun. It was high tide and the creek and green meadows looked quite beautiful.

The ride out to the bay took longer than I'd pictured, but we got to talking after a while and the time passed pleasantly enough. I told about moving houses with my dad, and Sandy seemed to be impressed, but Freddy acted bored. Then he told a story about his dad and my dad that I'd never heard before, but was pretty funny. It wasn't the kind of thing my dad would want to admit, but it wasn't glamorous enough for Freddy's dad to have made up. He said that when our dads were younger they used to sneak into Ken Hickman's cow pasture, where the cows would all be close together, sleeping. He said cows sleep standing up, so they would pick one near the outside and give it just the tiniest little shove, and over it would go. He said it wouldn't wake up till it hit the ground, and when it did it would let out the most surprised "moo!" you ever heard. They called it "cow-tipping." They gave it up after they tried it on a black angus bull that was just dozing, and collected his wits before he lost his balance. Sandy thought it sounded too cruel to be funny, and it did sound mean, but still, Freddy and I nearly died laughing when we pictured our dads doing it. And Sandy even got to laughing after a while. It made us seem real close together, all that laughing, and even though it sounds corny, it made me think there might be a good side to all the stuff that happened. We sure wouldn't be gliding down the creek on a sunny day, we probably wouldn't have run into Sandy skinny-dipping, and as bad a scene as that had been, we wouldn't have been friends with her without it. After a while we didn't say much, just got hypnotized by the hum of the motor and the pretty scenery. I don't think Billy C. was much of a concern to any of us at that time.

When we got out to the mouth of the creek, where it enters the Delaware Bay, I got a twinge of fear—the bay looked a little rough, even though the wind wasn't too strong. Sandy and Freddy showed no sign of being nervous. Maybe they didn't recognize the danger, or maybe they had faith in my yachtsmanship. I certainly acted and talked more confident that I had a right to. Around Freddy I seemed like an expert, because I knew a lot of nautical terms and boat stuff, but actually I had no experience. When we got out into the bay a ways the rollers started pushing us around pretty good. They were only two or three feet high, which doesn't sound like much, but it is when you're in a small, leaky garvey, and they were very steep. The boat was flexing pretty good and making some squeaking and groaning noises. Now Freddy and Sandy looked alarmed. Water was coming over the bow each time we hit a wave. I wanted to turn around, but I didn't want to turn sideways in such seas, for fear they'd just come right over the side and swamp us, or maybe push the rotten sides right in. I tried to angle towards the left, where the curve of the shore came around, but not too much. I wasn't even thinking about Billy C.'s stash anymore, which was probably a mile and a half or two miles down the shore. It seemed like forever, but we finally got back in close enough to where Freddy could touch bottom with an oar. I figured I better try to turn back around toward the creek here, because if we sunk at least we could probably make it to shore instead of drowning. I was tempted to just beach the boat, but decided we wouldn't be in too good a shape stranded out on the bayshore with seven miles of mucky marsh to cross before we even reached hard ground, which

124

would be wilderness at that. A wave hit us dead sideways as we turned, but miraculously the boat rode up it pretty slick, though there was a fearsome flex to the side, and there seemed to be a lot more water in the boat afterwards. The motor could just about keep up with the following sea and stay in the trough. We made good time with the seas pushing us and were mighty relieved when we glided back into the calmness of the creek. The boat was leaking worse than ever from all the flexing, so I guess we wouldn't have lasted much longer in the bay. It wasn't so bad that two people working steady couldn't keep up with the bailing, at least.

When we got near Mosquito Point landing, which is less than halfway back to our dock, the right side board cracked loose from the transom and a lot of water started pouring in. Freddy and Sandy hopped up onto the bowdeck and I inched forward to try and keep the stern out of the water a bit, and I steered right up a little sluice about a hundred yards past the landing, on the same side. I wanted to rescue the motor as the boat went down, but I knew it was too heavy to lug across the marshes and all the way down Mosquito Point road. Besides, it wasn't even our motor. There was nobody crabbing at the landing, so at least we didn't have an audience to explain our activities to. When we climbed up out of the sinking boat, we found more soft, mucky marshes. We also discovered that two of the shoes had washed overboard, probably in the bay. One was Freddy's, and Sandy's remaining shoe was gone. Both of mine were still there. I offered her my shoes, but she said she wasn't in the market for athlete's foot. We got across the marsh, then down the road, which was pebbly dirt for the first three-quarters of a mile where it crosses the marsh, then turns into a narrow, pot-holed blacktop road when it gets to high ground and the woods. It's another mile or more through the woods from there to the Route 47 highway. Freddy's and Sandy's feet were getting chewed up, so we took a couple of breaks, and I lent Freddy one of my shoes for a little while. Finally we got to Route 47.

There was a little country sandwich shop/diner about a hundred feet away from where we came out. I didn't know Jack's number offhand, but I figured it must be listed so we went right on over, figuring he was the logical one to call. When we got inside Freddy ordered us a round of Cokes. Our muddy, bedraggled appearance caught the attention of the two old coffee drinking, cigarette puffing customers.

CHAPTER THIRTEEN

A Close Scrape

"Do you have a phone?" I asked.

"Right over there," said the waitress in a scratchy voice. She had white-blond hair and had apparently smoked a lot of cigarettes herself over the years, or done a lot of shouting, because her voice sounded like pieces of sandpaper rubbing together.

"Local call?" she rasped.

I said yeah, and she handed me an old black phone from behind the counter. Then I had to ask for a phone book. Finally, I found the number and got through to Jack's wife, who then went out to the barn and got him. I told him to come on down to "Cafe 47" and pick us up and I'd have some good news for him. He didn't sound real happy, but said O.K.

"That Jack Pugh you were talking to? You must be low on options if you gotta call Jack Pugh for a ride," the waitress said. "You related? Maybe that's it. That's the only reason I ever heard anybody give for keeping company with him voluntarily."

I said thanks for the use of the phone and went and sat down with Freddy and Sandy. Just then a bad-tempered, sweaty looking guy, wearing a dirty apron, came out of the back, I guess from the kitchen.

"They eatin' anything?" he asked.

"Just Cokes," the waitress said.

Things got quiet while eight eyes stared at us. It was real uncomfortable. After a while the man said, "You kids ain't in any mischief, are you? How about we have some names. Might be a good idea to call your parents. You wouldn't have any objections, would you?"

"Oh, this is a private club?" Sandy asked. I nearly slid under the table. She sure had nerve. "I thought this was a public restaurant. My mistake. I should have noticed how luxurious it is and realized it was an exclusive country club."

"I think maybe you and your friends better take your business elsewhere, Miss Smarts. Somebody ought to turn you over their knee. Now git, you kids." I thought about the gun in the back of Sandy's pants. I hoped it was still covered. What if this guy saw it and called the cops?

"Our Uncle Jack will be here in a couple of minutes," she plowed on. More like a couple of hours the way he drives, I thought. It was a smart move about the uncle bit, though. It made us seem less suspicious. "We'll just sit where we are. If you want to turn me over your knee when Jack Pugh gets here, we can just see what happens."

"That's who they called a minute ago," the waitress said. "Old Pugh." I couldn't tell if that had an effect on the man or not. I was for bailing out, but I could tell Freddy and Sandy definitely wanted to stay put, so I just kept mum.

It seemed like Jack would never get there, and when he did he looked kind of startled to see Sandy sitting with us, but he didn't say anything.

"These kids related to you?" the man behind the counter said in a tone much more pleasant than the one he'd been using with us, but a little phony sounding.

"What's it to you, hash-slinger? You workin' for the Census Bureau?" Jack said curtly.

"That young lady could use a lesson in manners," the hash slinger said, somewhat less pleasant. "And I happen to own this place, clamdigger."

"Congratulations, pig-face. And I never dug a clam in my life. You better concentrate all your brain power on fryin' eggs. Don't go wasting that scarce resource worrying about young women's etiquette. Your parole officer wouldn't like it. Just shut your trap and mind your own business, greaseball."

The guy looked so mad that I thought he was going to burst an artery any minute. His face was red and veins were popping out of his neck and forehead. But he didn't say anything. Jack turned and started walking out as if he'd just been talking about the weather. He never batted an eye. I could see where he got his reputation for speaking his mind, and why a lot of people didn't like him.

When he got outside, he said, "Who's the new recruit?" looking at me.

"Sandy Spinelli. She already knows something about it," I lied. I could tell Jack wasn't fooled, and I was sorry as soon as I said it.

"Glad to see we're keeping a tight lid on our information. What's the big news?" We were standing in the parking lot, and I expected the cook to come out any minute armed with a meat cleaver, but Jack never even glanced behind him.

"Well," I said, "we went out and got our boat back, and tried to go out and get Billy's stash, but the boat started leaking in the bay—it was pretty rough—and we had to ditch it up a sluice by Mosquito Point. We let it sink, motor and all."

"We didn't have enough trouble, so you had to go dragging this young girl into danger. Then you go out on your own and try to drown her, and yourselves along with her. What's our next move, general, swap our shoelaces for live electric wire?"

"It was my idea," Sandy said.

"Oh, a new general."

"Joe didn't want to bother you because he thought him and Freddy had caused you enough trouble with your boat sinking and all."

"They didn't sink it. And they didn't kill that old hermit."

"Yeah, but if Billy C. did sink it, Joe felt like it was his fault for getting you involved. Anyway, he didn't want to do it, but I pressured him."

"I guess if I was his age you'd have a hard time making me say no to you, too."

"Besides, I have a gun. If we saw Billy C., I was going to shoot him." Freddy and I gulped in disbelief.

"Good plan," Jack said. "You and Joe should join forces with your plans. You could come up with some real winners. So—you shoot Billy C. and go to prison. He's the bad guy. He should go to prison. Young girls oughtn't kill people if they can help it. If anybody shoots Billy C., I'll do it. Life in prison ain't a real big threat to me. But we ain't gonna shoot him. It's better we get the goods on him and turn him in, so justice is served. But now we gotta act fast. He's really gonna have a hornet up his ass when he finds his boat's gone. Pile in."

It was nearly two o'clock when we left the diner, so I was worried when Jack pulled out and headed towards his house. I didn't want to be too late getting home, and I had already had enough adventure for one day. But I didn't want to cross Jack anymore, either.

"Tide's out," Jack said. "Won't take us ten minutes to fly the old Stearman out there and land it on the beach. We'll grab that stuff up before anybody misses us. Still plenty of gas in the old ship."

My heart started thumping. As fun as the last trip was, I didn't know if my guts were up for another one, especially landing on the beach. I knew he'd want me to go, not Freddy or Sandy.

"Can I go, too?" Sandy asked.

"Only two seats and I'll be in one of them. Joe didn't wretch his guts out on the last right, so I better take him and not risk a green horn. Young Chance and you'll hold up the windsock when we land. Try to stay out from under the trees this time, Chance. As long as you're holding the sock I promise not to hit you."

After the usual nerve-wracking ride up to Jack's, we got out and Sandy looked amazed when she saw Jack's plane.

"Where'd you get that thing, from the Wright Brothers?" Jack didn't seem to notice or care about the comment. "I wish the old lady was home," he said. "She's pretty strong when it comes to pushin' around that airplane."

"C'mon, Jack, we can do it," I said. "There's four of us." We pushed it out in the open without too much trouble, and Jack went all over the plane giving it his squinty-eyed "pre-flight inspection", as he called it. In the time since I first went up in the plane, my mind had pretty much erased the terrifying thoughts of it, to a point where I had been just about ready to fly the thing myself. Now, as I climbed up into the front seat and Jack handed me a pair of goggles, I had butterflies in my stomach, maybe even small birds, and my palms were sweaty, which is what always happens when I'm in a particularly uncomfortable spot. If the plane wasn't so chipped up and greasy looking, with the instruments—some with cracked lenses, and some with duct tape helping to hold them on—strapped to the struts that went up to the upper wings, and didn't smell like spilled gasoline, maybe I wouldn't have those pictures of crashing and burning flashing in my mind. "Clear prop,"

132

Jack yelled, and my heart jumped up into my throat. Rhnn...Rhnn... Clunk, Pop... Broppp—Broppp—Roar! The engine came to life and the plane started rocking. Jack revved it up and down so that the tail came up and went down, and then we started moving with the engine at about one-third throttle. Down to the end of the field we went, bumping and rocking. At least I knew what to expect when we turned around at the end of the field and roared back the other way and just cleared the trees taking off. I was a little more familiar with what was happening as we flew along, banked and turned, still climbing, but some of it seemed like I hadn't done it before. This time there was no roaring low down the creek, we just flew to the mouth and out over the bay. When we saw where the stash was, and that the blue tarp and stuff was still there, we circled around and got back a ways, and started dropping down along the coast line heading away from the creek towards what was probably a big piece of beach from the ground, but looked about the size of a long coffee table from up in the plane. We got down real low like we were almost going to hit, but were coming at it crooked and the plane was kind of wagging back and forth and up and down a little bit. Just as it looked like we were going to land, Jack hit the throttle and we started heading back up again, which was O.K. by me, since the left wing, the side away from the bay, was down awful low and we were crooked and wagging, like I say. If felt good to be back up in the air again, and I figured maybe Jack had decided the beach wasn't big enough. But he circled right back around and stared on down again, this time banking way over to the left side as we descended. He straightened it back up a

133

bit as we got close in and touched the left wheel down first, sending the sand flying and coming to a stop just before the beach got too narrow.

We climbed out and that ground felt pretty good, even if it was in the middle of nowhere. Jack marched right to the stash as I got my bearings and fell in behind him. We pulled off the brush and the tarp, and uncovered the metal box and a couple of rotten looking blankets and some rotten clothes. Jack had a little prybar in his hand, but we found that the box wasn't even locked. We unfolded the blankets and clothes—two pairs of dungarees and a flannel shirt—and in one of the blankets there were four coffee cans full of pot. There was nothing in the pockets of the pants and shirt.

In the box we found some files, one of which was Billy's school records, which weren't too impressive, and some school bus repair and maintenance records, which Jack said was probably there by accident. There was a Rolex watch, a Middle Township High School class ring with initials—not Billy C.'s—some pot pipes, a cover from "Reader's Digest Condensed Books—*Gulliver's Travels*—with what Jack said were bloodstains, and a bank account number written on the inside and also a safety deposit box number, and a key with the same number taped to it. Jack ripped the key loose and put it in his pocket. There was a wallet with an AARP card and a social security card, both with "Frederick P. Leaming" on them. When I saw that I remembered the rest of *Gulliver's Travels* back at Butterfly's house. It was real spooky seeing this stuff. Jack would hand me each thing as he got done with it.

"The pieces of the puzzle is falling together," he said real stern. We found Billy C.'s birth certificate, five one-hundred dollar bills folded together, a notebook with "Lawyer-Norton Rothman—881-4141" written on the front, and Playboy-type pictures torn out of a magazine and stuck here and there between the pages. On the back page it had some names of girls, most of which I didn't recognize, except 'Sandy Spinelli' and 'Katie Bass'.

"Prob'ly his girlfriends or drug customers," Jack said.

"I don't think so," I said. "Sandy Spinelli is the girl who came with us, and Kate Bass is my sister." I was kind of mad that that was the first thing he thought.

"Prob'ly girls he'd like to get in the sack with," Jack said.

I said, "That's a real nice way to put it, Jack." He just squinted at the list. I felt like you do when somebody dies, just a real heavy, low feeling. It was disgusting to think about Billy C. writing these names down and apparently robbing and killing Butterfly. It seemed like Sandy had a good idea in a way about shooting Billy C., if she meant it, but it was also real depressing, just like all this stuff Jack and I were finding out, and it seemed like there was no solution, just like the whole world was going to hell. Down in a corner of the box was a razor with no blades and a hunting knife with blood stains around the hilt.

"He might-a skinned a rabbit and got them bloodstains, and dripped them on the book, but I'm willing to bet that ain't the case. If them bloodstains turn out to be human, and we add in the victim's wallet, and that Gulliver book, which you can identify, we'll be a long way towards proving our case. And them bank numbers might be Leaming's too, though he don't really seem like the type who'd have a safe deposit box.

"We'd better gather up our loot and get airborne. We've spent entirely too much time. We should'a just scooped it up and done our inventoryin' back at the barn. But that's my fault. Anyway, let's hustle." I threw the coffee cans into the box, closed it, and we walked back to the plane. We saw that the tide was a lot higher. I set the box on the lower wing because Jack said we had to hop to it getting the plane turned around. The sand was soft and it was a lot of work for us to spin it around to face the other direction. Jack said normally you could do it with the engine, but this beach was too narrow with the tide up. Jack climbed up into his cockpit and turned the engine over. But it was real sluggish and would barely move. So he had me climb into my cockpit—there was a starter button up there but no key. He had me adjust my seat ahead so I could push down on the brake pedals, which was still a good long reach. He said to push on the brakes and turn the starter while he turned the propeller. I was afraid it would start and chop him up, but it didn't move a whole lot better with him helping it.

"She's still hot," Jack said. He took off one of his shoes and filled it with bay water and threw the water on the engine. Then he took both shoes and did it, so I climbed out, and he watched me take off my shoes and fill them with water. As soon as I straightened up, he put up his hand casually and said, "that's enough—no need to overdo it." I said, "You could have told me before I filled them with water." And he said "I was still decidin'." Then he went and filled his shoes up again, threw the water on the motor and put them back on. So I put mine back on. He had his squinty look, hands on hips, and kept looking at the water, which was rising, then back to the plane.

"Now what?" I said.

"She's gotta cool down," was all he said. "Too much compression." Every once in a while he'd give the propeller a try to see if it moved any easier.

"Don't never touch a prop like I'm doin', boy. Old Sam Wimley done it once on his Stearman. Positive ground. Pushed it a couple of inches. Don't you know she fired off about three cylinders. All nine had'a caught'n Sam would'a looked like coleslaw. Scared him as it was. But these is extreme times." Then he lapsed back into silence, the tide rising and the sun setting a little more every minute. I kept looking at our runway, which was slowly disappearing. But Jack wasn't the type to panic. I knew it wouldn't be dark for a few hours, but the runway would be gone long before then, and the plane might wash away if the tide got high enough. Here we were, miles and miles from nowhere. No water, no tent to keep off the greenheads and mosquitoes, and Jack just standing there squinting.

"Climb in. See if she turns over," Jack said after a good while, as though the critical second had arrived. He marched over to the propeller and stood at the ready. I pushed the starter, Jack pulled on the propeller. It slowly turned one revolution, then slowed almost to a stop. Jack scrambled up into the cockpit and punched his starter button and fiddled with the choke as the engine spun around and fired. It picked up a couple more cylinders and pretty soon was firing on all of them. Sand and water were flying from the prop, and the left tire was starting to get wet in the surf. The tail end of the plane came up a bit and the plane started to spin to the left, toward the bay. I could feel the pedals under my feet and realized I was still pressing on them a bit. I let up, and I could feel the right brake and right rudder pedal being pushed down and the plane swing back to the right a bit, then a little more, till it actually angled away from the water. Then we started moving a little bit. My heart was in my mouth again as I looked ahead at our reduced runway. We started to get some speed up and the sand was really flying. When we got to the end of the sand I thought we were going right into the bay, because we were on kind of a point of the shoreline, but the plane lifted up a bit and we skimmed along the surface for a ways, throwing a spray of water now with the prop. The bay looked rough beneath us. We had begun to lift off a bit when I heard the engine sputter, and we dropped down a couple of feet. I don't know if it was the water that did it or what, but I thought we had finally bought the farm this time. Then, like a miracle, the engine smoothed back out, one of the sweetest sounds I've ever heard, and we started climbing back up again. Jack climbed pretty steep, I guess maybe to get away from the water, and we angled left over the cove and towards Jack's field. I thought that by now Sandy and Freddy figured we were goners. It felt so free to be floating along up there after being stuck in that sand. The wings and their support struts and wires looked real sturdy in the dimming light. It didn't seem like the plane had any lights, now that it was getting duskier, or if it did, Jack didn't turn them on. The engine made a nice, steady, deep-sounding throb. And the ground below extended in every direction and looked lovely. I was feeling pretty good when Jack tapped on my shoulder and blasted in my ear, "where's the box?" My stomach dropped to my shoes. I had left it on the wing. I looked down but knew it wouldn't still be there. I didn't turn around and look at him right away. I could feel my head getting real hot, even with all the wind blowing on it. I was trying to think of a way to explain it, but I knew Jack wasn't much of a sucker for a sales pitch. All the harrowing effort we, and mostly Jack, had gone to, and I forgot and left the stinking box on the wing. I felt the plane bank real steep and swoop down, retracing our route for the short time we'd been over the marshes, but I knew it must have fallen off in the bay when we first got airborne. We went back to the beach, but we didn't see it, even though the tide couldn't have come up much higher in the couple of minutes we'd been aloft. I was burning up with shame and anger at myself. Jack had found the boat, found the box, gotten us on the beach, gotten us off, and all I'd had to do was get the box from the ground into the airplane, and I'd messed it up. I couldn't imagine what kind of stuff Jack was thinking or was going to say when we got back.

It wasn't long till we did. Sandy, Freddy, and Jack's wife were standing out in the field waving, Sandy was even jumping up and down a bit as we circled around to land. It was dusky, but you could still see fine, and Freddy was holding the windsock up on what must have been one of Mrs. Pugh's clothesline props. It was good to be landing as we bumpety-bumped in, but I was full of awful dread about what I'd done. We taxied up to the barn with the three groundlings tagging along till we spun around and turned off the engine. I just sat in my seat.

"Do ya have it?" Freddy shouted.

"Nope," Jack said. "Fell off the wing"

"Who put it on the wing?"

"Doesn't matter," Jack replied. "Wasn't nobody's fault. We had a tough time getting off that beach. Wasn't no time to be fooling around. I told Joe to set the box down on the wing and hop to helping me turn the plane around. After that there was too much to worry about getting started and underway to worry about an old metal box."

I didn't remember him telling me to put the box on the wing. Jack didn't seem like one to make something up, but I guess he was trying to take the weight off my shoulders, and I sure appreciated it.

"What was in the box?" Sandy asked.

"Everything we needed to convict our man," Jack said. I still didn't have the gumption to say anything. "The important thing is we know he did it, even though we don't have the physical evidence. It's a long way from a hunch now. I'd bet my tail on it, though I guess that ain't much of a wager."

"We were worried to death," Mrs. Pugh said. "These kids were hangin' around lookin' nervous, and after a while I noticed the plane was gone. Then they told me you'd gone out to find some evidence in a murder case. We were sure you two were corpses, too. So you think that boy murdered Fred Leaming?"

"Who doesn't know about this?" Jack asked. "Maybe we better hire some billboard space in case somebody ain't been told." I couldn't believe Jack hadn't even told his wife. At least I had Freddy to confide in. How in the world could Jack keep it all to himself without busting. He sure was different than anybody I'd ever run across before.

It was almost completely dark out, and I knew our moms would be worrying. We had to think of something. We had to call them because they would definitely be upset by now. I was sure my mom had called Freddy's or vice-versa.

"I'm gonna call my mom, Freddy. Any ideas on what to say?"

"Yeah. Say you been out flyin' with Jack Pugh."

"Don't worry about me," Sandy said. "I told my mom I was going to the boardwalk with Gloria, then probably staying over. My mom and hers can't stand each other, so I doubt they'll be talking. I told Gloria I was going out so she won't call and give me away."

"Maybe we could say we're camping," Freddy said.

"Yeah, but we didn't get permission, and it's already eight-thirty."

I had never before pulled a stunt like this on my parents. My dad would be mad, I knew, but would get over it. But my mom would be more disappointed than mad, and that's the worst on your conscience.

CHAPTER FOURTEEN

Leon

Both Freddy and I were in pretty hot water after that episode. Since we were up at Jack's and had some time to think, we were able to cook up a variation of what really happened, but which didn't give our game away. We said we found a boat at the creek and launched it. We said we took it for a row, but we lost one oar and the other one broke, then we began to drift down the creek with the out-going tide, which they know gets very strong. We said the boat started to sink, but we finally paddled it with our hands to the banks near Mosquito Point. Then, we said, we trudged out to the highway where Jack chanced to see us and thoughtfully drove us home. We didn't mention Sandy, since she had planned a little better and had a story for her parents, so why take a chance on giving her away.

We got grounded, and a bunch more things, including a long and grueling lecture by my dad, but all in all we came out of it fairly well compared to what we were scared might happen. But of course we were in real deep as far as Billy was concerned, and I was almost just as glad I was grounded, figuring that since he knew that I knew about his stash, that I was as likely as anyone to have taken the boat. My mom and me got to talking about Leon Berman, after I admitted I hadn't gone to see him. You know how it is, even when you're in trouble, the tension eases up after a while, especially when it's just you and another person alone for a while. We had a nice talk about things, and I admitted I could stand to be nicer to Leon. A while later my mom said I could break my punishment to go see Leon, but I had to promise to only go there, and definitely not see Freddy.

I was so nervous about Billy C. that I suggested my mom take me there in her car—it's less than a mile—to make sure I wasn't up to any monkeyshines. I called Leon, and he said sure, come on over. When I got there, his old aunt and his grandmother both looked at me pretty cool-like, but his grandfather—Pop, as Leon called him—was cheerful enough. Leon had a big bedroom that he spent a lot of time in. He had a lot of plastic models—cars, airplanes, battleships and stuff. His grandfather helped him with the bigger ones. They were all perfect, not all busted up like the few I had, and quite beautiful to look at. He had a butterfly collection, and the butterflies looked rather gruesome with the pins, which looked like huge spikes compared to butterflies, pierced through them. He had a big coin collection, which was neat, a big stamp collection, which was a little boring, a lot of plastic soldiers and dinosaurs, a chemistry set, some pickled specimens like frogs and cow's eyes and stuff and plenty of other things. But with all this stuff his room was still real depressing, like the rest of the house, grand as it was. I could just picture Leon in there messing with this stuff, hour after hour, getting more lonesome all the time. He had a collection of prayer cards from funerals that his aunts had saved for him. They were grim and sad, though some were written in kind of a pretty way. It sure seemed like an odd thing for a young boy to collect, but I found myself drawn to them—they were fascinating in a morbid kind of way. He also had Playboys he'd snuck from his "Pop's" office up on the third floor, and he was the only kid our age who had those.

After I got through looking at all his stuff, we were sitting around trying to find things to talk about when I found myself asking him if he could keep a secret. I felt like the blabber mouth of the world, but it was all I could think of, and I had to tell somebody. And somehow I thought he could keep the secret. Besides, he was smart, and maybe he'd have some ideas about how to straighten the whole mess out.

After I told him most of what happened, he just kind of went silent, and when I spoke again, he put up his finger, like he was thinking and didn't want to be disturbed. Then after a bit, he spoke up.

"Look," he said. "This Billy C. character can't be a hundred percent working alone. Somebody must know something. A relative or something. Let's think of his family or people who associate with his family. Like the Leeds up in Dennisville. They're pretty thick with the Tobins. They might even be related. My pop rounds them up on election day. Sometimes he sits back and tells me all about the old families around here. He says the rich ones split and moved all over, but the poor ones dug in deeper and deeper, and formed their own 'social network' as he calls it. They rely one another for all sorts of things, he says, because most people don't want anything to do with them. We ought to figure out a family who knows the Tobins pretty good—the Leeds or the Whelans or one of those tribes."

"Then what," I asked. "Ask them what they think of Billy C.? If they're so tight, they're not going to rat on one of their own to us."

"Well, they're not criminals. I doubt they're real crazy about Billy C. getting into so much trouble. It's bad for all of them. And he's no nicer to them than to anybody else, I'll bet."

"But what good will it do us?"

"Listen, Joe, you're in awful deep now. Short of calling the cops, the only thing you can do is hang it on Billy C. yourself, then call in the authorities. If you get one of those people who you can trust, you could tell him about all your evidence that you lost, and try to get him to come up with real stuff to back it up. He's going to have a more direct access than just about anybody. Since we've already had lunch, we've got a few hours where the old geezers won't miss us. Let's slip up to the Leeds' real quick and see what we can find out. If something doesn't develop pretty fast, I think you better call the cops, though, and take your chances."

I sure didn't feel like going anywhere, but Leon had two real nice bikes. One he got for Christmas, the other was from the Christmas before. Like I say, he had a lot of stuff. And all real nice. I don't know if it was because he was bored or what, but he was sure ready to jump right in with me. We went down to his basement, which was set up with a huge set of Lionel trains, among other things, and slipped out the back cellar door. His bikes were in a shed by the barn, and we jumped on them and headed out

146

his back driveway, then right on up Route 47. I was scared any minute we'd run across Billy C., but we were tearing right along on those ten speeds, and I figured that as long as he was on foot, we could outrun him. I was almost as scared my mom or dad or Mr. Chance or somebody would see me.

On the way up Leon had told me how he and his Pop went up to talk to the Leeds just before last election day. They lived in a big old farmhouse that looked like a total wreck. It belonged to one of his Pop's friends, and he rented it to them. They mostly got by on muskratting, laurel picking, firewood and pulpwood cutting, and such close to the earth enterprises as that. But Mr. Leeds was having a lot of trouble paying the rent, so he went and took a job down at the fish docks in Cape May. There's eight Leeds kids from up older than me down to little babies. Leon said it was so far for Mr. Leeds to go in his old broke-down car that he would often stay down in Cape May all week, sleeping in his jalopy and coming home just on Sunday evenings—he worked seven days a week at the job. Leon said he missed his kids so much, especially the little ones, that he'd come home Sunday nights and pile all the kids and his wife in the car so it would be real cozy. Lots of times poor people like their cars better than their houses, Leon said, because they don't have the bedbugs and varmints, and they are easier to keep warm. Anyhow, they'd all pile in and ride out to Mosquito Point, which was near their house, and they'd stay up all night, 'cept the kids, who would doze off a good deal, and Mr. Leeds would always have the two little ones in his arms, 'cause he missed them so much. And they'd stay that way looking

147

out at the stars all night, with him holding those kids. Then when the sum would start to come up, he'd take and drop them back off at home and head back to Cape May for work.

I had seen the Leeds kids in school off and on. They didn't attend regularly, and they always looked a little starved and wild, and had the most raggedy clothes you could imagine, but they did stick together. If somebody was picking on one of them, which happened a lot, it wasn't long before a couple of other ones found out. and they'd put up a mighty good stink. Getting thrown out of school wasn't much of a threat to them, so they'd do almost anything if things got out of hand. Mostly they didn't though. Kids would just back down and call them dirty names. and they'd look real sad and forlorn once they'd calmed down. But I never really thought about what they might be like out of school. Leon seemed to know a lot about them.

"They're pretty good people at heart," Leon said. "They're smelly and dirty and all, and live pretty primitively, but that doesn't mean they're dumb or have no feelings. They're mixed up fairly close with the Tobins— Mrs. Tobin is a Leeds or something—and so they must know basically what's going on. And I don't think they would approve of what Billy's up to. They wouldn't be likely to call the cops on him—it's a kind of a code of honor—but they probably wouldn't lie for him, either.

When we got to the Leeds house, a bunch of kids were in the yard, and they looked startled to see us, but not unfriendly. Leon marched right up and knocked on the door. I hung back a bit—it was a scary looking place, back off the highway about half a mile on a dirt road through the woods. It was a big abandoned farmhouse, covered with tired out red insul-brick, with an even bigger barn out back. There were cars in the yard—one upside down—that would have made good antiques if they weren't so blown out. A lady that looked like she was from the movie "Tobacco Road" answered the door. She had long, gray hair and rotted out teeth. "Hi, Leon. How's your Pop?" she said.

"Hi, Mrs. Leeds. Oh, he's O.K." Leon said. "Mr. Leeds around?"

This lady looked beat, but she couldn't have been much older than her forties.

"Ned's out cutting laurel. Should be home any time. "C'mon in and have a cup. Who's your friend?"

"That's Joe Bass. The house mover's boy."

"Oh, yeah. Powerful man, that Joe Bass. They say he beat a Percheron horse in a pullin' contest wunst."

"I never heard about that," I said. "But dad doesn't tell me everything." I knew it wasn't true, but I didn't want to be rude.

We went in and it looked like some real sloppy young boys' clubhouse, but bigger. The furniture, what there was, was all torn up, and there were stacks of things all over. There was an outboard motor and a chainsaw apart in the kitchen. The bathroom had no door, and no plumbing, either, except a big sink had a pitcher-pump alongside it.

There were a couple of bikes in the living room, a kid's pedal car, some guns, axes, knives, and all kinds of dangerous stuff around that the kids didn't pay any attention to, though they stuck to me and Leon real close. The old lady and an older daughter were cooking on a real woodburning kitchen range. They had water boiling and made us some coffee in old, scarred-up looking McDonald's mugs. Everybody drank coffee, even the little kids. Everything seemed real unsanitary, but I drank the coffee down as best I could, again not wanting to be rude.

"We came here to see if you can help us out," Leon said. He was quite confident with people, not like I'd expected.

"We'll do what we can," Suzy said.

"A friend of ours has got on the wrong side of Billy C. Tobin," Leon went on. "And we're pretty sure he killed a man, and did a lot of other things, like rape and drugs. This friend of ours can't even come out of the house for fear of running into Billy C. I know you folks are related by marriage to Billy C., and I was hoping you might know just what he's up to and who he's up to it with."

"Oh, I wouldn't know nothin' about that, Leon. And I don't aim to be runnin' afoul of no kin," Mrs. Leeds said. Leon had been pretty smooth, I thought, but this looked like a brick wall. Suddenly Leon's bright idea looked like a real bad one. Now she was going to tell Billy C. we'd been snooping around there after him.

"I might know somethin'." It was Mr. Leeds. I hadn't heard him come in. "That boy's nothin' but trouble. I'd

150

shoot him myself if I could get him backed into the right corner. But I can't, he's my sister's son. If she asked me to shoot him, it would make it a lot easier."

Mr. Leeds was a skinny guy, about five foot eight, with a very unprofessional haircut. He had reddish-blond hair, like all his kids, and a large but skinny head, and a scary looking face. His pants and T-shirt looked like he'd been wearing them for two months. He had on Acme brand sneakers with no laces, and there were a lot of big scratches, on his arms and ankles like he'd been in catbriars.

"That Billy C.'s been dealing drugs with some hoodlums up in Atlantic City," Mr. Leeds said. "He's selling them around here, and I'm afraid the kids is going to get mixed up in it. I'm pretty sure he killed old Butterfly Leaming, from what I've heard around. Him and Dicky Meehan's been stayin' out at the old Oddfellows Hall over in town. It's out there by the old train station at the end of Gatzmer Street, down around the corner where nobody can see them coming and going. What I was thinking was maybe me and the older boy ought to go up there with a hammer and nails and some kerosene. We'd wait till they went in and were asleep, then we could pour kerosene all around the outside, light it, and once it caught, nail the door shut—only the one opens anyway, and the windows are boarded up with plywood. Wouldn't they have a hot time, then? That's better than shooting them and leaving a body, and a lot safer."

"Maybe these boys could help you," Mrs. Leeds suggested. My mouth must have dropped open. I had expected Mrs. Leeds to pitch in and say what a crazy idea it was, and here she thought it sounded pretty good. Or seemed to.

"What's-a-matter, boy?" Mr. Leeds said, looking at me. "Don't you think he's got it coming? What-a you want to do, get him locked up by the law so he'll get three squares a day and clean sheets every night? We both know he killed the old man, and he'll do a lot more before he's through at the rate he's going. Remember Homer Whelan that got tangled up in his gill nets out in the bay? He was bothering Bob Slaney's retarded daughter. Then he started on Bob's little grandkids. Me and Bob seen him one day tendin' his nets. We let on we wanted to buy some fish off him so we didn't have to go home emptyhanded. We was just gonna club him over the head and throw him overboard, but we seen he was halfway through tending a net. So we tied our garvey to his'n, and when Bob got behind him, he threw that net up over him and pulled it tight around his arms, then we dumped him and pulled the boat farther up along so the weights would pull him down. We left his boat runnin' in gear and never worried no more about him. That's clamdigger justice, and it works real good. Now I aim to barbecue Tobin and his friend—I wasn't a-goin-to, but you say your friend's in a bad way with him, too, and that tips the scales of justice, far as I'm concerned. I seen old Jack Pugh, and Jack says the Tobin boy sunk his boat. I mentioned to Jack I'd heard Billy C.'d been hanging around that Oddfellows Hall, and he seemed awful interested. I doubt he'd have any complaints if he heard about the boy's well-done remainders turning up in the ashes o' that place. He holds his mud pretty good, does old Jack. Now, he's sunk Pugh's boat, killed old Leaming, is selling drugs, scairt your poor friend half to death, deviled with my retarded niece, Edna, and I'd say he's about ready to get his desserts. I don't blame you boys if you don't want to help—I don't 'spect it's in your line. But I don't want no blabber-guttin', neither. Nuthin' ruins a thing like this worse'n gettin' the cops involved.

Me and Leon just kind of walked out of there in a daze. I had thought Jack was a man of action, without much respect for authority. He was a Boy Scout next to this guy. We promised not to say anything, but I knew we had to. We couldn't just let this guy "barbecue" Billy C., even as bad as he was. And yet I knew it was a solution that had a lot of arguments in its favor. It was true that we hadn't gone to the cops because we feared they wouldn't be able to do enough; that Billy C. would either get off too easy or altogether. Leon said he was having a hard time coming up with arguments against the plan, too, but he said Mr. Leeds should use screws on the door, not nails, because hammering would make too much noise. It's funny how even the most gruesome ideas can have their practical side. I had been thinking the same thing.

"I wonder if he'll do it," Leon said. "These clamdiggers are often big talkers, but on the other hand, they do some amazing things from time to time."

"I have a hunch he's gonna do it," I said. "Something about the way he laid it all out, and the tone of his voice. And his wife going along with it. Maybe he has more of a beef than he told us. And if he's anything like old Jack Pugh, he ain't exactly scared off by a little danger or stretch of the law."

"It *is* the law as he sees it," Leon said. "Didn't you say that old Jack said 'if anybody's gonna shoot him, I'll do it?' And this guy pays a lot less attention to the laws as we know them than Jack Pugh does."

"That's who I ought to tell. Jack. He'll know what to do. I wouldn't want to call the cops and get Mr. Leeds in trouble. But Jack will know how to handle it," I said.

Just then Leon said, "Why do you think this car behind us is going so slow?" I turned around and there he was— Billy C. Tobin. And behind the wheel was Dicky Meehan —I thought he was in a mental institution or jail. I was so scared I almost fell off my bike. It was all I could do to keep my balance. They pulled up along side us and Billy C. said, "Wanna go for a ride, Joe? Who's your friend?"

CHAPTER FIFTEEN

The Oddfellows Hall

"Leon," I said.

"This is Dicky Meehan," Billy C. said. "He's a faggot. He likes boys like you. Myself, I like the young babes. Where you going?" We had stopped our bikes, and they'd stopped along side of us. I didn't really want to stop, but I couldn't make myself keep going. I was praying that somebody'd come by and see us.

"Oh, we're meeting my dad right up the road here," I said, trying to sound like I wasn't scared out of my wits.

"Don't lie to me, boy. Nobody's meeting you. Get in the car."

"No, I'd better not. My dad's waiting for me."

"Where's he waiting" We'll drive you there."

"That's alright, Bill."

"Get in, boy. And pencil-neck, too," said Dicky Meehan, flicking open a switch blade.

I knew it was the worst thing I could possibly do. I wanted to be a hero and run out and flag down a car, but I was so scared, all I could do was say O.K. I guess I figured if I stood up to him, the violence would start right away, and it was easier to put it off. Leon and I both got in the back seat. It was a two-door, so Billy C. had to

lean the seat forward to let us in. Once we sat down, Billy C. got out of the car and threw our bikes down into the ditch at the edge of the woods. The weeds were so thick nobody would ever see them. It sent an even deeper wave of fear up my spine and into my head, and I was so scared I didn't even think I could control myself. As we drove along I calmed down just a little. Leon broke the silence.

"Drop us off in front of Pedrick's, if you don't mind," he said.

"Let's ride around a little first," Dicky Meehan said. "I don't get much chance to drive my old man's car. He's in the hospital, and my brother's up at Fort Dix, so I have it all to myself." He seemed quite pleasant and conversational, and I wanted to believe he'd protect us. But I knew better. Especially when he said, "You boys snort coke?"

"No, Dick," I said, trying to sound definite.

"You ought to try it. Maybe if I have time, I'll get a chance to show you something.

Billy laughed at this, and I sunk lower in the seat in horror. I looked over at Leon, and he looked worse than scared. He looked like he was possessed. I don't guess I looked much better. I had often imagined being in situations of great danger and had thought of the brave or clever maneuvers I would pull to get out of them. But they were always dangerous situations like you see in movies, where you can kind of grit your teeth and plow through, not situations where lunatics have you in their complete control and have horrible, perverted things on their minds. I wasn't too aware of where we were going, but I did take notice when we turned down a road in the woods. It was narrow and bumpy, and branches were constantly scraping the sides of the car. Dicky and Billy C. were drinking beer and smoking joints, and at one point Dicky stopped the car and they both got out to take a leak. I thought of jumping over the seat and ramming the car into gear and taking off, but they were right close to the car, and I didn't think I'd have the time or the courage to pull it off.

I don't know how we got there, but after a while we came out near the railroad tracks in Dennisville. Dicky parked the car back up in the woods a ways, and we all got out. We went along through the laurel till we were directly across from the Oddfellows' Hall. There wasn't a house in sight, though off to the right, a long way off, you could see the crossing for Dennisville-Petersburg Road. We went across to the building, and Billy C. opened the door. He looked around and motioned us in. Once we were in, Dicky and Billy C. pushed a big, old kerosene stove in front of the door for a barricade. It was quite dark inside from having all the windows boarded up, and the plaster was falling from the ceiling. There was crepe paper and the remains of Happy New Year 19... at the far end over what looked like a stage and kitchen. There were old Bentwood chairs around the sides, and a lot of stuff that looked like it would burn good once it got started. They led us up a big staircase in the vestibule to what appeared to be their camp. Upstairs, there were two pool tables with long since defunct lights hanging low over the middle of them. On top of one was some blankets, and on the floor there was a sleeping bag. There were tons of candy wrappers and smelly hoagie and food wrappers, and a lot of beer bottles. It was very dim inside due to the windows being boarded up, so it was hard to see the whole place. In a big, dark closet, there was a ladder going up to the attic, where there was a window with no glass in it, just what looked like a rubber floor mat. Dicky went up there and was looking around. I wondered if Mr. Leeds knew about it.

I wondered if Mr. Leeds was going to come burn the place down. He had said he would wait and make sure they went in, but maybe if he heard their voices that would be good enough—why would he suspect anyone else was in there with him?

"What the hell we gonna do with these two, Bill?" Dicky asked.

"You mean after we find out where my stuff is? That's what they're here for. Who's the sissy, Joe? Ain't you s'posed to be with Freddy Chance?"

"I'm Leon Berman. And I'm not a sissy."

"We'll see about that," Dicky said.

"What's the story, Basshole?" Billy C. said. "Where's the boat? And where's the box?"

"That's what I want to know," I said. "Where is the boat? I ain't seen it in two weeks. Somebody's been messing around down by the creek. Old Jack Pugh's boat got sunk, and ours got stolen."

159

"Sunk, huh?" Billy C. said. "No kidding?" Him and Dicky looked at each other and kind of chuckled. "Now cut the bull. You're the only one besides Dicky here that even knew I had the stuff. Does that old man Pugh have an airplane? One day when I was out by the boat, an old fashioned plane with two people in it was buzzing around real low. From what I hear, the only one has a plane like that around here is that old buzzard, Pugh. Now how about it?"

"I don't know if he has a plane or not. All I know is he tried to blame Freddy and me for sinking his boat, and my old man had to go yanking it out just to shut him up."

"You ain't got no idea about my motor or box of stuff?" He sounded as if he was ready to believe me, and I relaxed just the tiniest little bit.

"He's lying," Dicky said. "Who else could have done it? Either this kid or somebody he told about it."

"Maybe you did it," Leon blurted out, looking at Dicky Meehan. They both looked at him like they were in shock.

"You said Joe and Dicky were the only ones that knew you had it. How was Joe supposed to get it without his boat?"

"Shut up, pussface. Nobody asked you," Dicky said.

"Maybe he's right," Billy C. said. "Maybe that wasn't Pugh. Or maybe you hired him. You're the one who said he had a plane. And you knew I'd moved my stash. But you didn't know where. What, did you want it yourself, Meehan?"

"You done too much crank, Bill. I don't know where your boat is or your stuff is. Cool out, man. Don't listen to these little idiots. Let's start giving them something to improve their memories. A couple of lumps on the head might help."

"Maybe you're right," said Billy C. "Maybe they're just lying."

"Who's more likely to tell a lie, Dicky Meehan or Joe Bass?" Leon asked. "Dicky's been in jail for stealing, he's been in the nut hatch. Think about it, Bill. What does Joe Bass have to gain taking your stuff, whatever it is? What would he do with it? Dicky's the one who would know what to do with..."

Thump!

Dicky kicked Leon in the side of the head.

"Why'd you do that?" Billy C. asked. "I wanted to hear him finish."

"He's full of crap," Dicky said.

"No, he's not," I said. I figured it was about time I did something brave. I just hoped it was as smart as Leon, and that I'd live long enough to finish saying it. "I saw Dicky hanging around the creek with Jack Pugh." Dicky went to hit me, but Billy C. grabbed him and threw him down, then held his arms behind his back.

"Let go," Dicky said. Billy C. let go roughly and said, "When was that?" I tried to remember when we went looking in Jack's plane.

"A little over three weeks ago. They went out in Pugh's boat. Another time, maybe the next day, I saw him in Pugh's car."

"He's lying!" Dicky said. "The little creep's making it up!"

"No, I'm not, Bill. You're my friend. You bought that motor, and then somebody stole the whole works. Why would I want to get you in trouble or take your stuff?"

"I took the boat," Billy C. said. "But then somebody took it off me. The only one that could have done it is Meehan."

"Nuts to you, Tobin! If you're so stupid that you believe these little idiots, the hell with you. I'm outta here."

"No so fast, boy."

Dicky started to walk towards the door, and Billy C. grabbed him. They stood there looking at each other, and I figured any second Billy C. was going to flatten Dicky. But Dicky reached into his pocket, and like a flash, whipped out a knife. It was the switch blade, and it flicked open as he brought it out. Billy looked stunned for an instant, then grabbed for it. It cut his hand when he reached for it, and as he drew it back in pain, Dicky jammed it right into Billy C.'s stomach. He let out an awful gasp and staggered back, but stayed on his feet as Dicky pulled the knife back out. Then, slowly, Billy C. sank down to a sort of sitting

162

position. He looked glassy-eyed and very astonished. Dicky stood there watching him a couple of seconds or so. Then Billy C. fell over sideways with a thud, and seemed to be unconscious. I was frozen, watching Billy C. turn from the scariest terror I'd ever known to a silent lump. And he'd been sort of sticking up for us. And Leon had him going. Now I was so scared I felt like puking. Then Dicky turned to us.

"And you," he said. "You little punks. I've killed one, so I won't be any worse off if I make it three. Now hold still while I kill you."

"Not necessarily," Leon said. "That was self-defense. This would be murder one. For all anybody knows, you came here to save us."

"Sure, jerk. Then you'd double-cross me again."

"So what if I did? You're not going to get away with killing all three of us."

"Maybe I will if I burn down the building."

That was logical, Dicky probably didn't even know how logical, and I went deeper into shock. I couldn't believe Leon was so cool-headed. He actually made Dicky stop and think, and meanwhile, I was so scared I couldn't have spoken a word if I wanted to. I knew then if I lived through this, I would never call Leon a sissy again.

"How is that going to help?" Leon said. "They'll still find the bodies. We're only half a mile from the firehouse. They'd probably have it out before it was barely started. And you've left evidence all over the place."

163

"Like what?" Dicky said.

"Like my Aunt Mildred rode by when you guys stopped us out on the highway. And she saw me. And she knows your dad's car. And plenty of other people saw us. And you have that bloody knife. If you leave it here, it might not burn. And if you take it with you, you might get caught getting rid of it. Look, Billy C. is our enemy, not you. We were just using you to get him riled and buy some time..."

"Like you're doing now?"

"...More or less. Anyhow, we're glad you stabbed him, and we don't care if you get in trouble for it or not. Why should we? We would have done the same thing if we had the chance. You're an intelligent guy. Do the smart thing. Don't set yourself up for the electric chair."

He was amazing. Dicky was standing there listening to him, and the longer Leon went on, the calmer Dicky got. I couldn't tell if he was buying it, but he was listening.

"Tell you what," Leon went on. "It would be better if the cops never found out you were in on it at all. Take that knife and clean it up. Wipe it for fingerprints, then leave it in Billy C.'s hand so his fingerprints get on it. Then gather up all the stuff that might link this place to you—me and Joe'll help you—and tie it up in one of these blankets and take it with you. Me and Joe will call the cops and say we found Billy like this. Even if we were to rat on you, which we won't, there will be no evidence to link you to this place."

Dicky just stood there looking from us to Billy C. for a while, and everything was silent. I could hear my heart pounding.

"Makes sense," he said after a while. "Get the bedroll off the pool table. I'll wipe the knife off on Billy C.'s shirt. He might not be dead yet, but he can't last much longer the way he's bleeding."

We got the crumpled bedroll down and spread it out on the floor. Dicky got some clothes and shoes and threw them on it, then started going through the beer and soda bottles and throwing them in the bedroll. "Fingerprints," he said. "I ain't sure whether or not to kill you guys. I feel like I might be getting shammed. But it don't hurt to get some of this evidence together before I go."

"You don't have to take all those bottles with you," Leon said. "Just wipe them for fingerprints." For the next fifteen or twenty minutes we went around wiping all the bottles we could find in the place with old rags of Billy C.'s clothing. I felt bad seeing Billy C. just lying there in a pool of blood, even as much as I hated him, but it was funny how after a while we sort of got used to it and walked around him like a sleeping dog.

"I think you're taking me for a ride," Dicky said after a bit. He went out and got the knife from under Billy C.'s hand. "If I kill you now, I got no witnesses to worry about. I just can't decide whether to have a little fun with you first or just get it over with." I had been thinking of getting the knife when Dicky wasn't looking and stabbing him, but I was scared he'd take it away from me, and Leon's plan

165

seemed to be working, whatever it was. Now Dicky looked real scary, like he was beyond Leon's clever talking.

Bang! Bang! Bang! It sounded like the building was being hit with a wrecker's ball. Then a screeching noise like the barricade was moving, and the door came open, and then my dad and Jack Pugh came storming up the stairs. Dad had a short-handled sledge hammer in his hand, and Jack had what looked like a shotgun. I felt like a hundred pounds had been lifted off my chest. But Dicky wasn't through yet. He snatched Leon up by the hair and held the knife to his throat.

"This knife's razor sharp. Anybody comes a step closer, and I'll cut his throat." They both stopped in their tracks, about twenty feet from us, and so did my heart—and time, as near as I could tell. I saw Jack, who was standing behind my dad, take his gun and level it across my dad's shoulder, aiming right at Dicky. He aimed carefully for a couple of seconds, and I expected him to say something, like "lay down the knife."

Blam!! With a flash of fire, the gun went off. Dicky's head snapped back, spraying blood and brains, and he hit the floor. Leon never moved a muscle.

"Pumpkin ball," Jack said calmly. "Didn't think I could miss from that close." Everything was quiet for a second, then Billy C. sat up with a groan.

Blam!! Jack let Billy C. have it with the other barrel.

"Self-defense," he said.

I guess Leon's ears must have been ringing for an hour. It was at least that long before he said anything. With the door open there was a fair amount of light, and it was the gruesomest scene you could ever imagine, with brains and blood all over. Even Jack looked a little shook. The police finally came, and it was a big ordeal to sort things out with them. It was the painfulest experience of my life. I couldn't count the number of nights that went afterwards when I couldn't close my eyes without seeing Leon standing there white as a sheet and Dicky flattened out behind him. My dad put a big strong arm around my shoulders, then the other one around Leon's, and it seemed like we stayed that way in a tight little circle till Leon's pop got there. It was a while before my dad and me were calmed down enough to talk about it, but we finally did begin to talk on the ride home.

"Son, how in the hell could you let all this happen and not tell me? Did you think I wouldn't help you? Did you think you'd get in trouble? I've aged twenty years in the last hour or so."

I told him I was afraid he'd call the cops, and Billy C. would get hauled in, then let out on bail, and then kill Freddy and me. It sounded ridiculous as I told him, but that's what I'd really thought. And in a way it did make sense. And I tried to explain how it got even more complicated as I got further into it. I wound up telling him about our secret boat and the trips with Jack and everything. And I told him to go easy on Jack, since he was only trying to help us, and we had dragged him into it.

167

"We better edit this a little bit before your mom hears it," my dad said. "Let's be a little more honest about what we're up to in the future, though, son, and maybe keep your eye peeled toward preventing such a mire from sucking you in."

Even though he was disappointed and upset and all that, he wasn't as mad at me as I'd imagined he would be. I guess he was glad enough that I'd pulled through O.K. When we got back to the house, Sandy and Freddy were there, looking pretty anxious.

"Go ahead and have your pow-wow," my dad said, after giving a brief account of what happened. "I'll lay it out for your mom as best I can, and we'll see how that squares with the account Freddy's given her. Meanwhile, you owe these two a thank you for lookin' out for you when you disappeared."

We went out back of the house, and I laid out what had happened with Leon and me. Then Freddy and Sandy took turns telling me how they figured out that I was missing and where to look.

It seemed Gloria's father had seen Freddy and me talking to Billy C. and Dicky by their car. But of course it had been Leon and me. He had casually mentioned it to Gloria, who had casually mentioned it to Sandy. Sandy knew Freddy and I were grounded, and also knew if it was us, we might be in real trouble. She called my house, and my mother told her I was at Leon Berman's. Then she called Freddy, who said it wasn't he, then she called Leon's. Leon's folks looked around and found that we weren't there, the bikes were missing, and they got pissed. They in turn called my mother, to see if we were there. My mother was mad about me sneaking out, but didn't realize the danger I might be in.

Meanwhile, Sandy came over to Freddy's, and they called Jack, who got real alarmed when he heard I was missing and may have been talking to Billy C. Jack told Sandy to call the police and my dad—both of whom he said to send to the Oddfellow's Hall. After calling the police, she ran over to my house and told my mom, who nearly laid an egg when she heard the cops were involved and I was in danger. My mom then got hold of my dad, because she knew the house where he was working and called on the phone. The cops had to come all the way from Port Norris, so my dad and Jack knew they had to do something themselves because if the one cop on patrol was tied up there was no telling when he'd get there.

Now Jack knew Mr. Leeds pretty well, and he'd been talking to him in a general way about Billy C. Mr. Leeds had told him about Billy C. camping at the Oddfellows Hall, and Jack must have figured that if Billy C. had done anything to me and Leon, the best chance of finding us or Billy C. was there. I guess my dad hadn't wasted any time getting over there, because he was all the way in Sea Isle and got there at about the same time as Jack. That's when they busted into the building.

We were all feeling gloomy about the two people being dead, although as Sandy said, it could have been two different people—Leon and I—just as easy. The cops asked us a lot of questions, and for a while we were afraid Jack might get into trouble for shooting Dicky and Billy C., but in the end they just closed the case. We wanted to do something, but we couldn't think of what, until Jack came around and said he'd turned in the key to the safe deposit box, which I had completely forgotten about, and the police found six hundred dollars in it. Butterfly didn't have any insurance, so the county had buried him, and there was only a temporary marker on his grave. My dad called the Surrogate's Office in Cape May Court House, and asked if the money could be used to buy Butterfly a gravestone. The surrogate said it was not exactly the way things were done, but in light of the circumstances he freed up the six hundred dollars and Freddy, Sandy, Leon and I all rode our bikes down to Bayshore Monuments and picked out a stone. Mr. Lewis, the owner, asked if we had any ideas about what to put on the stone. He gave us a pen and paper, and we puzzled around a bit. Finally we came up with an epitaph:

Frederick P. Leaming
Slipped into God's arms,
May 27, 1985.
He never hurt anybody,
and had a kind heart for cats.

Leon had the prayer card collection, of course, and was very helpful with the epitaph. We felt good about the gravestone, but still couldn't shake the gloomy spell. When we were almost home, I said, "What about Billy C. and Dicky?"

"The Hell with them," Freddy said.

"You're probably right," Leon said, and I kind of gulped. "If there is a Hell, Billy C. is definitely there. And most likely Dicky Meehan, too. But they were human beings." We had stopped our bikes and were hanging around in front of Pedrick's, hardly realizing we had stopped. "And they shouldn't just be forgotten."

"Let's go see if Mr. Lewis has any damaged or cheap stones," Sandy said. "If we chipped in a couple of bucks apiece, maybe we could get two real small ones."

We rode back and I asked, "What's the cheapest stone you have," and explained our predicament. Mr. Lewis said he had a couple of flat stones that were meant to be used as markers at the foot of a grave, but had been laying around for a long time.

"When these two get buried, I'll see that they get a little something if their families don't provide any," he said. "No charge."

"And we have to give you their epitaphs," I said. "You still have that piece of paper?"

He looked a little impatient and a little amused.

I wrote:

> *Dicky Meehan. Died July 11, 1985.*
> *God help him.*
> *Then Leon took the pad:*
> *"Billy C. Tobin. Died July 11, 1985.*
> *No comment.*

I felt like a weight had been lifted off my heart as we rode our bikes home. We had looked out for Butterfly and found his killer. And we had looked out for his killers, too.

Rather than causing Leon to be cooped up even more, this caper seemed to have the opposite effect. He came over on his bike more freely, and he and I and Freddy spent a lot of time puzzling over the whole episode and trying to get it to make sense. We didn't have much luck, but Leon came the closest. We were all celebrities for a while, especially Jack, but he wanted no part of being famous. I got teased a lot about my "girl friend" Sandy, especially by my family, but she was real cool about it. She wasn't too good to stop and talk to us guys, like most high school girls, and always seemed to be worried about what Leon and I had gone through over at the old hall. It was a "trauma" she said, and we shouldn't take it lightly. So we didn't.

It was hard to believe that both Billy C. and Dicky were dead. And that Jack had killed them. He was never any different afterward than before as far as I could tell, and when someone tried to make a hero out of him—like the Kiwanis or the newspaper—he just sent them packing with a few choice words. The only thing he said to me about it was, "You shouldn't oughta get into cars with people like that. Don't be afraid to make a stand when things get bad. You can't learn that till you've been in a bad spot, like you was. But now you know." That was it. And my dad didn't lecture me too bad on it either. But my mom brought it up a good deal, and I could see it shook them both up quite a bit, and Katie too.

A lot of nights went by before I could shut my eyes without seeing Dicky's head snap back when the gun went off, or seeing Billy C. gasp and collapse as the knife went in him. Even though they were such rotten characters, I guess their deaths still rattled me quite a lot. I was glad, though, that old Butterfly hadn't died without making a ripple, and that the guy who murdered him didn't get away with it.

The End